Ben pulls himself out of the h[...] He's wearing plain navy-blue [...] rippled with perfect muscles, li[...] marked all over with scars. So many of them. Violating his beautiful body. The scars of his childhood. They hurt me as if they are my own. I feel like there's something I need to do. Not just for me, but for both of us.

"May I hug you?" I ask Ben.

His shoulders tense. "Now?" he asks.

"Is that okay?"

He inhales uncomfortably. "I don't think it's a good idea, Erin."

"Please." I look into his eyes, desperate. "I *need* to do this."

Ben holds my gaze for a long time, then he exhales and says, "Do whatever you need to do."

Maybe I'm not ready for this or maybe I am. I don't care. I swim across the hot tub and climb up onto the seat. I stand in front of Ben, afraid to touch him, afraid of how it will feel. My heart races. My breaths quicken. My body trembles. All I can think about is fear. *I HATE that fear.*

I need to do this now, even if it kills me.

I close my eyes and wrap my arms around Ben as tightly as I can. He wraps his arms around me just as tightly. I feel our hearts pounding. I feel our chests rise and fall. I feel the heat radiating from his skin to mine. But I don't feel *any* pain.

I stay there in Ben's arms. Until I stop trembling.

Praise for LOST IN LOS ANGELES:

"I have read many books and I don't think one has moved me as much as this one did ... My eyes are welling up and my heart aches. I absolutely love this book."
—Elizabeth, The Bookish Way

"Lynne made me feel like I was right there with Erin, feeling everything she was. Her pain was so real and it broke my heart ... You have to read this book! Trust me ... The ending will blow you away."
—Susan, Susan Loves Books

"A beautiful story about finding the will to live again ... It has definitely won one of the slots for my favorite books."
—Tiffany, Goodreads

"I found myself falling in love with Ben and Erin and the city of LA."
—Vanessa, Goodreads

"I'm an emotional mess right now ... Wow ... This book is a must read. Highly recommended."
—Denise, Goodreads

LOST IN LOS ANGELES

J.W. LYNNE

This book is a work of fiction. Names, places, organizations, programs, businesses, incidents, etc. either are products of the author's imagination or are used fictitiously. All characters appearing in this work are fictitious. Any resemblance to actual persons, living or dead, is entirely coincidental.

Copyright © 2013 by J.W. Lynne.

All rights reserved.

Except as permitted under the U.S. Copyright Act of 1976, no part of this publication may be reproduced, distributed, or transmitted in any form or by any means, or stored in a database or retrieval system, without the prior written permission of the author.

ISBN-13: 978-1494997687
ISBN-10: 1494997681

To my mom, who taught me, among other things, to love books

009**LOST IN LOS ANGELES**

Chapter One

My high heels dance across the sticky hardwood floor of the narrow, unlit hallway. The smell of vomit mixed with beer hangs in the air. By sheer luck, I dodge a puddle of something—I'm not sure what. My vision is so blurred that it's hard to appreciate much of anything. I'm pulled through a doorway that I almost walk past.

"This is it," Barry says.

The room that we enter is illuminated only by slivers of street light streaming past the edges of the closed blinds. Crumpled clothes blanket the floor. The framed photos on top of the dresser and nightstand are in disarray, as if they were dumped there like trash. The place looks remarkably lived-in considering that Barry just moved here last week.

"Do you have a t-shirt or something?" I ask. I don't really want to sleep in my prom dress, although at this point, I'm tired enough that I feel like I could.

"Sure." Barry opens a drawer and tosses me a faded t-shirt that is starting to rip along the bottom seam.

It isn't appropriate for me to change clothes in front of Barry. "Where's your bathroom?" I ask.

He points to a door, and I stumble toward it. Without Barry's hand to hold, walking is harder, especially in high heels. He laughs. I laugh too.

Once I make it into the bathroom, I sit on the toilet and pull off my shoes. Then I realize I have to pee. I open the lid, slide down my panties, and sit back down just before the almost unending tinkling begins. Afterward, I feel better.

I wash my hands and then try to slide the zipper of my dress down my back, but it won't move. I think about asking Barry for help, but that would mean he would see me in my underwear, and we're not ready for that, so I wriggle the dress over my head. My skin burns where the cloth scrapes it. I hang my dress and my bra on the hook by the bathroom door, slip on Barry's t-shirt, and look at myself in the mirror. Without Barry's muscles to give it shape, his t-shirt drapes over my body, falling almost halfway down my skinny arms. The curls I forced into my long, sandy-brown, usually-unruly hair an hour before my father dropped me off at the prom are somehow still cascading perfectly down my shoulders, the way hair normally does only in magazines. The tiny bit of makeup I tentatively applied is still there too. I look pretty, but like a little girl, not a woman. I lift Barry's shirt to my nose. It smells like him. I smile. I haven't felt this happy in a while. I take a deep breath and open the bathroom door.

Barry is sitting on his bed. He is now undressed except for his boxers. His muscles bulge out everywhere. His shoulders. His chest. Down his belly. And his body is excited. I suddenly become aware of the fact that Barry's t-shirt barely covers my bottom. I'm sure he can see a hint of my lacy, black panties. I try to shake away the fog that envelops my brain as Barry stands.

"Is that what you're wearing to bed?" I ask. It's a ridiculous question, but I can't think of anything else to say.

"No." He slips off the boxers and walks toward me.

Anxiety tingles through every nerve in my body. I try desperately to sober up. "Barry, I don't think we should …"

He raises an eyebrow. "Should what?"

"*Do anything.*"

"Why not?" He sounds genuinely curious.

"This is our first … uh … date." *It's not exactly a date.*

"Come on, Erin. We've known each other since kindergarten."

He's right; we have. When we were in elementary school, Barry and I were friends. We'd go on adventures together, like "bug expeditions" where we'd lift logs and rocks to find the insects crawling underneath and "building expeditions" where we'd construct entire villages out of twigs. Our friendship was innocent, even including the one time before today that I saw him undressed: when we were eleven years old and we snuck into the playhouse under the slide in his backyard to show each other our private areas. Barry had asked to see whether I looked anything like the naked girls in the magazines that he found in his father's tool shed. After I lifted up my t-shirt and lowered my shorts and underpants, Barry said I didn't look anything like those girls, which made me feel disappointed. But then he added that my body was "nice and normal-looking." He showed me his private area too, just to be fair.

In junior high, Barry grew into everything I wasn't. He became confident, good at sports, and popular. We each found our own separate group of friends, and those groups barely acknowledged the other's existence. I felt like Barry and I would still be a great team, if only we were on the same team. But we weren't anymore.

Now, with high school behind us, I wonder if Barry and I can be friends again. We will be going to the same college this fall. It would be nice to have a friend there. Maybe even a boyfriend.

I look down at Barry's excited body, even though I'm trying not to. "Let's just take things slow."

Barry grips my upper arms and looks into my eyes. "How slow?" he whispers.

"I'd feel better if you were wearing clothes."

Barry lets go of me, a little roughly. He grabs some

fresh boxers from an open drawer and pulls them on. "Are we good?" he asks, sounding frustrated.

"Yes," I say. "Thank you."

He leaps onto the unmade bed and pats the spot next to him. Hesitantly, I lie down, my back to him. His strong hands take hold of my shoulders, massaging them. "I just, you know, wanted to make this a special night," he says.

"Tonight *was* a special night." *Better than I ever imagined it could be.*

Our prom feels like it was days rather than hours ago. I went alone because the friend who I was planning to go with had to fly out to Michigan for his grandmother's funeral. I was weaving past green tissue-paper streamers hung in honor of our prom theme, "The Wonderful World of Oz," when I tripped. A hand stopped me from falling. It was Barry's.

His date for the prom—one of the many girls he dated during high school—had gotten sick at the last minute, and so he'd ended up at the prom alone too. When he told me he missed our "bug expeditions," a happy ache filled my chest. He asked if I wanted to dance. And then we did. A slow dance. It was magical, even though my pulse was pounding so loud in my ears that I could hardly hear the music.

We spent the rest of the night reminiscing about high school from our completely different perspectives—his, as a jock, and mine, as a geek. It was the first time we'd really talked since elementary school, and we connected in such an amazing way that I felt like the past six years had disappeared. I assumed he felt the same way when he invited me to a prom afterparty that he and his friends were throwing on the roof of the New York City apartment building they'd just moved into. The party was the wildest one I've ever been to. There was alcohol everywhere. In fact, I couldn't find a single non-alcoholic drink. I probably drank way too much, but I hardly felt the effects of the alcohol because my head was already light and dizzy from the thrill of having Barry's arm around me as we wandered under swaying strings of white lights, looking out over the quiet rooftops of a city asleep.

I roll toward Barry, so that we are lying face-to-face. He moves forward and gently kisses me. *Our first kiss.* His lips ease mine open and his tongue enters my mouth. He tastes like beer. He brushes my hair from my face and his lips move down my neck. He slides a hand under my shirt and fumbles over my chest. His other hand hooks over the top of my panties and eases them down.

"Barry," I say.

He kisses me again on the mouth, thrusting his tongue into me.

I push him away. "Barry!"

"What?" He sounds annoyed.

I take a breath, trying to compose my thoughts. "I like you. I really do. But I don't want to do that tonight."

His eyes narrow. "Then why did you come to my room with me?"

My cheeks flush with heat. "Because neither of us is sober enough to drive me home."

"I offered to get you a cab," he argues.

I hadn't wanted to take a cab by myself at three o'clock in morning. And also, I'd thought that sleeping next to Barry, waking up with him, and having breakfast together would be fun. Now I just want to get out of here. "Okay, fine. I'll take a cab," I retort.

He shakes his head. "You know, it's not right to get a man all worked up and then ..." his tone changes to a high-pitched, whiny one "... oh, no, I don't want to do *that*."

I feel a bit guilty. Maybe I was being naïve by coming to Barry's room with him. But mostly, I feel angry. "I'm just going to go," I say, getting to my feet.

Barry grabs my arm and yanks me back onto the bed. His body falls on top of mine, forcing the air from my lungs.

"No," he says coldly. "No, you're not."

Chapter Two

Barry's hand touches my shoulder. I shove it off and scream, "GET AWAY FROM ME!" I don't care who hears me. I am too angry to care.

Something is covering my eyes. I claw at my face to get it off … until my eyes are uncovered … and I take in my surroundings.

My stomach clenches tight with humiliation.

I'm not where I thought I was—in Barry's room. I'm on an airplane, heading to Los Angeles, trying to get away from the nightmares that have haunted me for the past few months, even when I'm awake.

A flight attendant is peering down at me, his forehead furrowed. "Miss, I need your seatback in the upright position in preparation for landing," he says, his voice gentle.

"Okay," I mumble, raising my seatback and shoving my eye mask into the pocket of my sweatpants.

Around me are staring eyes, but they look away before I make eye contact. I open the window shade and let my vision adjust to the bright sunlight reflecting off the tops of the puffy clouds below us. Even though I learned in physics how planes are able to fly, it never fails to amaze me that something so heavy can stay up in the sky just by continuing to move forward.

Suddenly, everything outside the window goes white. Seconds later, the world beneath the clouds is revealed. Tiny houses line serpentine streets. Many of the homes have a sparkling blue pool in the backyard. I spot some palm trees. There are mountains in the distance. This place is so different from where I came from. I hope *I* can be different here too.

The plane dips a few times and then hits the runway harder than it should. The woman sitting next to me gasps. I don't. For the past two months—ever since that horrible night with Barry—sensations have felt different than they used to. Either I am extra-sensitive to them or I feel numb. Right now, I feel numb.

Panels on the wings come up to slow us down, and the plane fights against the air. I like this feeling because it's strong enough to cut through my deadened senses, if only for a few moments. I want to feel *something*. I want to feel like I'm still alive.

As the plane slowly rolls toward the terminal, a woman's voice over the PA system welcomes us to Los

Angeles. I keep my face turned toward the window even though there isn't anything of interest outside now. I don't want to look at the woman next to me. After my outburst at the flight attendant, she must think something is very wrong with me. I don't want to see her eyes searching my face, trying to figure me out. I don't want to risk having her ask me if I'm okay, because I can't tell her the honest answer: I'm not.

* * *

The airport shuttle van drops me off in the parking lot of a tired-looking motel. The place looked slightly better in the pictures online, but not much. The driver tosses my suitcase onto the concrete in front of me, and it promptly topples onto its back. He doesn't bother to make an attempt to right it. I tip him anyway.

As I wheel my suitcase into the cramped motel office, the balding man behind the desk looks up. "Checking in?" His tone is inappropriately pleasant for such a sad place. I sense darkness beneath his closed-lipped smile.

"Yes," I say, stilling my shaky body. I don't feel safe here.

"Credit card and photo ID," he replies.

"I called ahead. I'm paying cash." I offer him my driver's license.

He studies my ID with a smirk. "It's fifty a night plus a two-night deposit."

On the phone, I was told that the rate was forty-five dollars, but I don't dare argue. I pass him the cash, and he hands me a key attached to a beat-up metal tag with the number "9" printed on it in chipped black paint.

"Stay as long as you like," he says, "but you need to pay each day by noon or you'll be considered checked out." Then man stares at me without speaking long enough that I figure he's done with me.

"Okay. Thank you," I say, and then I leave.

Room Nine is right next to the murky-green motel swimming pool. When I unlock the door, I'm met by the smell of stale cigarettes in my non-smoking room. There are so many stains on the dingy, brown carpet that it almost looks like it was designed that way. I pull my suitcase into the room and close the door behind me. I can't lock the deadbolt, because there isn't one. I can't fasten the door security chain, because the chain has been torn right out of the doorjamb. I shudder when I imagine how that might have happened. I wonder what my father would think if he knew I was staying at a place like this. I guess he probably wouldn't care.

I march back to the motel office, bringing my suitcase with me.

The man barely looks up as I approach his desk. "Checking in?" he asks.

"No," I say. "I was just here. I just checked in, but my room smells like smoke, the carpet is filthy, and the security chain is broken."

"Right," he says. "They're all like that." He places a dusty pine-tree-shaped air freshener on the counter. "This will help. Enjoy your stay."

It takes a moment before I realize he's serious.

"I'll be checking out tomorrow morning," I say.

I wish I could check out right now, but I don't know where to go. Just over a year ago, when I came to Los Angeles with my best friend, Star, we stayed at a swanky hotel on Hollywood Boulevard. Her dad paid for it. I don't have enough money to stay at a place like that now. There aren't many places that I can afford on my own.

I leave the cardboard air freshener on the desk, and I walk out of the office. I just want to go to sleep, but I haven't eaten all day. I'm not hungry, but I shouldn't go to bed without eating something, so I lock my suitcase inside my room and head back outside.

As I approach the sidewalk in front of the motel, I sense the distant aroma of grilled onions. After following it for more than a full block, I find the source: a truck parked in a supermarket parking lot. A menu is scribbled on a whiteboard near the back window. The bean and cheese burrito is only two dollars. I order that.

The man inside the truck ladles beans onto a tortilla, followed by some salsa. He sprinkles shredded cheese on top, folds the burrito like he's done it thousands of times, and wraps it in foil. I hand him two dollars, and he hands me the burrito. His eyes are kind, but I don't let his gaze hold mine for long.

"*Puede sentar allí,*" he says, gesturing to a folding table and two plastic chairs.

Even though I took Spanish in school from seventh grade on, I'm not certain of what he said. Maybe it's because of his accent. Maybe I'm too tired to think. He might have been offering me a seat.

"*Gracias,*" I say, for the burrito, and for the possible seat offer.

I sit on one of the plastic chairs, open the foil wrapping of my burrito, and bite into the soft, doughy tortilla. The beans, cheese, and salsa spill into my mouth, awakening my taste buds. *Oh wow, this is so good!*

For the next five minutes, I see nothing, hear nothing, and feel nothing other than the burrito I devour. I finally lick my lips clean and toss my crumpled foil into a trashcan.

"*Fue bien?*" The man asks me if I enjoyed my meal.

"*Sí. Gracias,*" I reply.

Feeling refreshed, I head into the nearby supermarket. Mexican music blares through the speakers overhead. In the produce section, I collect an apple and two ripe nectarines. In the cereal aisle, I pick up a box of store-brand breakfast bars. On the way to the checkout area, I pass a 75-percent-off clearance rack and grab a pair of 25-cent flip-flops that I will wear, instead of going barefoot, in my motel room.

Thinking about the motel brings my mood plummeting back down.

I choose the self-checkout lane, because I don't want to interact with anyone, but the clerk at the 20-items-or-less line waves me over. I force a smile and bring my basket to her.

"Did you find everything okay?" she asks as she scans my items.

"Yes," I say. Since we're already talking, I ask, "Is there somewhere around here where I can use the internet?" I need to try to find a decent motel for the rest of my stay in Los Angeles. I can't imagine spending more than one day in the place where I'll be staying tonight.

"There's a public library on Franklin and Hillhurst." She draws a little map on the back of my receipt.

The library isn't far from here, but it's already almost seven o'clock, and I don't want to be out in an unfamiliar neighborhood after dark. I decide to go to the library tomorrow.

Tomorrow I will find a new place to stay.
I hope.

* * *

Morning sunlight streams through small holes in the saggy drapes, making my motel room appear even more pathetic than it did yesterday. The battered wooden table, chair, and nightstand are tightly wedged in a row between the door and the bed frame. I arranged this makeshift barricade last night, hoping it would be enough to keep someone from entering my room, or at least provide me with a warning if they did.

I slept fitfully overnight, not enough to face the day, but I must face it anyway. A good thing about this room is that it's so unpleasant that leaving it to go out into the world is preferable to staying inside. And so I eat a breakfast bar and a nectarine, get dressed, and drag the furniture far enough away from the door that I can escape.

The air outside is cool. On the sidewalk in front of the motel, an expressionless woman wheels a blanket-draped stroller. A middle-aged man with tattoos covering both arms and part of his neck nods his head to the beat of the music blaring through his headphones. A foul-smelling man with his hair in disarray picks through a trashcan. He places his finds gingerly into his bulging plastic bag before he walks on. I head in the opposite direction. Soon, I am in a funky neighborhood of trendy clothing stores and atmospheric eateries, the kind of neighborhood that Star and I always sought out. I wish we'd discovered this one during our visit to Los Angeles.

A sweet, welcoming smell wafts from a tiny coffee shop. Inside, a few customers are scattered throughout the claustrophobic space. Everyone is alone, but not alone, preoccupied with their various electronic devices. I'm relieved that no one seems to notice when I enter.

The cheery girl behind the counter smiles as I approach. "What can I get you?"

"A small coffee," I say.

"Anything else?"

"No, thank you." The fancy muffins and pastries are too expensive for my budget.

"That'll be a dollar eighty-five." We exchange money, and then she asks, "What's your name?"

For an anxious moment, I think she's about to make conversation, but then I notice her orange marker poised above a paper coffee cup. "Erin," I answer, holding my breath until she finishes scribbling down my name and turns away.

When she turns back, she hands me a warm cup of coffee with my name on it. "Enjoy, Erin. Cream and sugar are on the left."

I dump a few packets of sugar and plenty of cream into the coffee and swirl it until it turns a uniform light-brown color, then I choose a plush purple velvet chair that faces away from everyone else, plop down on the chair, and gaze out the window. Well-dressed people stroll along the sidewalk, mostly in pairs. I focus on the eclectic shops and restaurants on the other side of the street. I could explore them, but I won't. Not without Star.

Suddenly, my vision blurs. Tears fall down my cheeks. *I've been in L.A. for less than 24 hours and already I'm failing miserably at my purpose here.* I'm supposed to be happier than I was in New York. I should feel far away from my pain, but it is still inside me. It doesn't help that I'm staying at a motel where I don't feel safe, in a city where I know no one. I guess most people who feel this way would call home and talk to someone. But there's no one back home—actually, I'm pretty sure there's no one in the world—who deeply cares about me. No one really cares whether I live or die.

I pretend to sip my coffee until no more tears come. Then I dry my eyes on a napkin, grab another napkin just in case, and head to the door.

As I deposit my trash in the wastebasket, I hear a man's voice, "Excuse me."

I'm not sure whether he's talking to me, but even if he is, I don't care. I don't want to talk to anyone. I keep walking.

A hand touches my right shoulder. I spin around and find myself looking into the dark eyes of a stranger. He's about my age, tall, and muscled, the kind of guy who could easily be threatening but, oddly, I am struck by an overwhelming feeling of calm. Looking at his face comforts me in a way that I haven't felt comforted in a very long time.

"I think you dropped something," he says, pointing to the purple chair where I was just sitting. On the chair is my camera case, dark-blue with glistening silver stars on it. I rush over and exhale with relief when I find my camera safely inside its case.

By the time I turn around, the guy has returned to his laptop.

"Thank you," I say so quietly that he probably doesn't hear me. And then, without looking to see if he has a response, I walk out the door.

* * *

"I thought you were checking out today," the man behind the motel office desk says, barely hiding his characteristic smirk.

"I changed my mind," I say. The truth is, after spending over two hours on a library computer searching for somewhere else to stay, this motel seemed like my best option. The others were either too expensive or poorly located.

I hand over the day's room rate.

"Enjoy your stay!" The man smiles broadly and, for the first time, I notice that some of his teeth are sharpened into points, like fangs.

"Thank you," I mumble, trying to hide my horror, and I leave.

I walk away from the motel and turn north, toward Griffith Observatory. The observatory sits high on a hill overlooking Hollywood. I've visited it only once before—with Star. I'm not sure if I'm ready to face the observatory now, but I don't give myself a chance to reconsider. I focus every bit of my energy into my footsteps, trying not to think at all.

I'm sweating by the time the bright-green observatory lawn stretches out in front of me. Families picnic on blankets set on the grass. A gray-haired couple poses for a photo. A younger man and woman stroll, holding hands. I pass the serious-looking concrete men that encircle the base of a towering spire and approach the imposing observatory building. My skin prickles with anxiety, but I ignore my apprehension and pull open the heavy entry door.

Inside is a vaulted atrium, its ceiling adorned with fanciful painted images of animals and people against a backdrop of blue sky. When I first saw it, I thought it was beautiful, like something from a dream. Now, looking at the bright painted ceiling makes me feel weak and lightheaded.

I lean against the circular wall in the center of the room for support. Below me is a pit where a bronze pendulum swings back and forth. I focus on the gentle swinging, letting it calm me, until the rod at the bottom of the pendulum hits one of the pegs in its path and the peg falls down. A docent begins to explain how the pendulum works, but I don't stay to listen. I don't want to see another peg fall.

When I turn away from the pit, the atrium is packed with more people than a few minutes ago and they seem to multiply by the second. The echoing noise of their chatter rings in my ears. My heart races. My breaths come fast and deep. My vision is fading into black. I half walk, half crawl to the perimeter of the room and sit on the floor, my back pressed against the cold wall. People stare at me. I try not to care. I force myself to breathe, counting in my head as I inhale and exhale: *One Mississippi, Two Mississippi, Three Mississippi. Three Mississippi, Two Mississippi, One Mississippi. One Mississippi, Two Mississippi, Three Mississippi. Three Mississippi, Two Mississippi, One Mississippi.*

After a few minutes, I am calm enough to rise to my feet. Still leaning against the wall, I breathe: *One Mississippi, Two Mississippi, Three Mississippi. Three Mississippi, Two Mississippi, One Mississippi. I can do this. I just have to keep moving.*

I let go of the wall and start down the left corridor. If nobody touches me, I'll be okay. *Please don't anyone touch me.* I walk slowly, but with purpose, carefully dodging distracted tourists, keeping my body away from others.

Without warning, someone darts in front of me. I swerve to avoid them, and something grazes my right forearm. Intense pain courses through my entire body, as if someone has cut into me with a dull knife. The people around me continue on their way as if nothing happened. Anxiously, I look down at my forearm, afraid of what I will see, but I find no wound. *There was no knife. None of my blood has been spilled here.* I rub my arm to take away the sting.

Over the PA system, a woman announces something about a demonstration of the Tesla coil. All at once, people surge toward me. *I'm trapped. I can't escape.* Bodies hit mine. Burning pain stabs me from every direction. I want to scream at everyone to get away from me, but if I do, they will think I'm crazy. Maybe I *am* crazy. I once read that if you think you're crazy then you're probably not, but I don't know if that's really true.

I press myself against the nearest wall and close my eyes, desperately trying to go numb. But it's too hard. My body feels like it's on fire. I force my eyes open and put every ounce of my concentration on the Tesla coil—a monstrous metal thing in the center of a wire cage, behind a wall of glass.

Suddenly, lightning bolts emanate from the coil. The crowd murmurs with delight and moves toward the glass. Empty space forms in front of me. I hold my breath, pull myself away from the wall, and race to a door marked "Exit." It shuts behind me, leaving me outdoors, in the sunlight.

I should feel less claustrophobic now, but I don't, and I won't until I face my memories, maybe not even then. I find the familiar walkway lined with tall, white arches that runs along the side of the observatory building. Tree-covered Griffith Park stretches out below, its winding dirt trails dotted with hikers.

I locate the exact spot where Star and I once stood to

pose for a picture, where we threw our arms around each other and turned toward the camera, cheek-to-cheek, wearing goofy smiles. That picture was the wallpaper on my phone until two months ago. After that, it was too painful to look at.

I imagine myself climbing up onto the wall that separates me from the ground far below. I balance on the narrow edge and look down. My hands and feet tingle, and my head swims with vertigo, but the anxiety that has been plaguing me melts away. I feel at peace.

I leap into the air, and for an instant, I rise. I am flying. Then gravity takes over, pulling me down. I plummet toward the Earth. Falling fast. I should be scared, but I'm not. Dying can't be more painful than the life I'm living, even if dying hurts like hell. And it does hurt. When I slam into the hard ground, the agony is indescribable, but it only lasts for a moment before the world goes black. And it's over. But not for long.

I awaken from my nightmarish daydream, disappointed that I'm not dead.

I've been thinking about dying a lot lately. I want to be rid of the sadness that hangs over me like a suffocating fog. This trip to L.A. was supposed to help. My visit to Griffith Observatory with Star is one of the best memories I have, but when I try to remember what it felt like to be happy with her, I feel only guilt. I struggle to picture her smiling face, but the image instantly fades into a very different image. One that will haunt me as long as I live. I see Star in the driver's seat of her father's car, her head slumped to the side, her eyes half-open, and her soul gone.

Chapter Three

I toss the cellophane that once held a tuna sandwich from the Café at the End of the Universe into a Griffith Observatory trashcan. I bought that sandwich because it was past dinnertime and I hadn't eaten anything since breakfast.

I should probably do a preemptive pee and head back to my motel. I want to get there before the sun sets. I don't want to be caught outside in the dark all alone.

A sign indicates that the nearest restrooms are through an opaque glass door. I push open the door and find myself in a massive underground two-leveled chamber that I didn't know existed. My heart pounds in my throat, but unlike earlier today, the feeling isn't completely overwhelming. Sometimes it's easier to enter the unknown than the known.

As I walk toward the restrooms, I glance at the meteors displayed along the wall. They look so much like ordinary rocks that it's hard to believe they came from outer space. Back when the meteors were lying on the ground somewhere after having fallen from the sky, I bet people walked right past them, never realizing how special they were.

At the end of the walkway, right by the restrooms, is a stairway that leads down. After my pee, I descend into an expansive room with photos of stars covering one wall and a model of the solar system overhead. Boisterous children play on scales designed to tell people what they would weigh on different planets. I slip past them into a quiet alcove containing a large drum labeled "Seismograph." On the wall are readouts obtained during various earthquakes. As I read the description beside them, something lands by my side. I whip around, but I find not a some*thing*, but a some*one*: a little girl. The wispy, golden curls in her hair bounce.

"Did I scare you?" she asks me.

Am I so fragile that this tiny child actually frightened me? "You *startled* me," I say, my heart still pounding from the burst of adrenaline.

"Sorry," she says, her innocent eyes looking genuinely remorseful.

I force a smile at her. "It's okay."

"Hey!" she exclaims, pointing to the seismograph drum. "You made an earthquake!"

I shake my head. "I don't think so." Then I look at where she points. There is a small blip from just seconds ago.

"Do it again!" she urges.

I jump—not expecting anything to happen—and another "earthquake" registers on the seismograph. Bewildered, I read the description. Apparently, this drum measures vibrations from a sensor in the floor. I point to tile below me. "There's a sensor under there," I tell the girl.

She scoots over next to me and jumps up and down, but the seismograph needle doesn't move. She's just too small.

"Let's do it together," I suggest.

"Good idea!" she exclaims. "Ready! Three, two, one, blastoff!"

We jump.

The little girl checks the seismograph and then bounces with joy. "That was COLOSSAL! Let's do it again!"

I smile. "Okay."

"Three, two, one, blastoff!" she shouts.

We jump and she giggles. I laugh too. I haven't laughed since …

"Eliza!" A woman grabs the arm of the little girl and yanks her away from me. "You can't go around bothering people."

The girl lowers her head. "Sorry, Mommy."

"She wasn't bothering me," I say. "She's a great kid."

"Thank you," the woman says, but it doesn't sound like she agrees with me. She turns back to the girl. "We're leaving."

Eliza looks up at me, her eyes filled with so much sadness that my heart aches. "Bye."

"Bye," I say reluctantly.

I watch them walk away until they disappear into the crowd, then I crumple onto a bench, feeling suddenly drained. In a time that feels like it was long ago, I wanted to be a kindergarten teacher. I imagined having students like Eliza, spunky and curious. The thought of sharing knowledge with children and inspiring them to discover new things once excited me. Maybe it still does a little.

I glance at my watch. *It's getting late!* The sun will set soon, if it hasn't already. I sprint upstairs and dash outside. The sky is filled with pink and purple clouds that look more like a painting than something real. Instead of stopping to admire them, I run across the observatory lawn, which is now sprinkled with people and portable telescopes. My sneaker catches on the edge of the sidewalk and I fall onto the pavement. Blood oozes from one of my knees.

"You okay?" a gray-haired man asks.

I'm crying again. *I hate crying.*

The man crouches down next to me, examining my injured leg. "Doesn't look like you'll need stitches or anything," he says. "Can you move it?"

I bend my knee and then straighten it.

"Good. Let's get you up then." He offers his hand.

I don't want him to touch me. I don't want anyone to

touch me. I quickly scramble to my feet, before he can assist.

"Care to have a look at the moon before you go?" he asks, gesturing to his telescope.

"I'm kind of in a rush."

"The sky is crystal clear tonight." He cocks his head to the side. "It'll only take a minute."

I'm not sure how to politely extricate myself from this situation without looking through his telescope, and so I walk over and peer into the eyepiece, remaining wary of my surroundings.

Instantly, I am unbelievably close to the moon—a perfect gray circle pockmarked with scars from many past traumas. I pull myself away from the eyepiece and look up at the glowing moon in the evening sky, then I look back through the telescope, studying the moon's scars one by one.

"My turn! My turn!" a young boy says from behind me.

I step away from the telescope and the boy rushes forward to take my place.

"Pretty cool, huh?" the man asks me.

"*Extremely* cool," I say. "Thank you." The sense of wonder that has been reawakened in me is so strong that I think I might cry again. I turn away from the man before I do.

At another telescope, a long-haired guy wearing an

R2-D2 t-shirt invites me forward. Through the eyepiece, I see Saturn. As I stare at its rings, I notice a few brilliant stars close by.

"The stars near Saturn are so bright," I whisper.

"Those are actually moons," the guy says to me. "Saturn has tons of them, and there are probably more waiting to be discovered."

"Wow," I breathe.

After a good look at Saturn and some of its moons, I thank the guy and go to the next telescope, and then another one, and then another. By the time I've gazed through every telescope on the lawn, I've seen planets, stars, and Orion Nebula—which the matronly woman with the telescope described as "a baby star nursery."

Even though it's late now, I feel a bit less tired than I did before. And a bit more alive. But then I realize something, and my heartbeat quickens.

Now I must do what I'd been desperately hoping to avoid.

I must walk home in the dark. Alone.

* * *

I slink through the shadows cast by trees in the moonlight. I hate shadows because they hide things. Usually, there's nothing inside shadows but darkness, but there could be something horrible—at least according to the horror movies Star and I used to watch. We saw practically every one that came out, because we liked being scared. Being scared is fine when you're safe in your best friend's living room and have nothing to fear, but when there's actually potential real danger, like right now, it sucks.

I round a bend in the trail and spot a skinny dog ahead of me. He has no leash. There's no owner in sight. When he turns to look in my direction, I see that his eyes are wild. There were signs along the trail warning of coyotes. *He must be a coyote.* To my right, I sense another pair of eyes: a second coyote. I assume there are more here, hiding in the shadows, but even if there aren't, I'm already outnumbered.

Maybe they'll run off if I start walking again. I take a few careful steps, but the coyotes don't budge. I feel more eyes, getting closer. Something boils up inside me. Fear. Anger. Rage.

"GET AWAY FROM ME!" I scream so loud that my throat hurts.

The animals stare at me. My heart pounds against the inside of my chest.

I slam my feet into the ground, so hard that I feel like my bones might break. "GET … AWAY!" The first coyote bounds off into the shadows. The one on my right disappears also. All of the eyes I felt are gone in an instant. But I continue pounding my feet against the ground, smashing the pain inside me into the earth. Tears stream down my cheeks. "GET AWAY! GET AWAY!"

Suddenly, a group of people—who look like they're

about college-age—appear from around the bend. They assess me with narrowed eyes before glancing around to see who or what I was screaming at. There is nothing and no one there.

"Crazy," one of the girls says under her breath.

"What did you say?" I growl.

"She said you're crazy," another girl says, cocky.

I get right up in her face—surprising even myself—and I scream, "GET AWAY FROM ME!" The girl moves back, spooked, and I run past her, screaming as loud as I can, "GET AWAAAAAAY!"

I run fast through the darkness, my throat throbbing and my shins aching. The longer I run, the more the hurt grows. But I don't stop running. Despite the pain, I feel better than I've felt in a very long time. Better than I ever thought I could feel again.

* * *

Although it is well into nighttime, the funky neighborhood where I had coffee this morning is still very much awake. I walk past lighted windows, peering into the shops and restaurants. I try to stay hidden in the shadows because I don't look very presentable. My t-shirt has a dirty, wet spot in the center, where I wiped the tears from my face as I left Griffith Park. I assume my face is streaked with dirt as well.

I slow down when I pass a café where friends and couples dine by candlelight. There's a soft murmur of happy conversation. I imagine sitting at one of the tables here with Star, sharing fries from a fancy paper cone and enjoying veggie burgers. For the first time in a long time, I'm actually hungry. I'd love to eat at this little café, but I don't want to sit at a table alone. And so I keep walking.

A few windows away, the coffee shop is buzzing. My purple velvet chair is now occupied by two people even though it's meant for only one, but I hardly register them. I am busy looking for the guy I met this morning—the one who told me I was about to leave my camera behind. Of course he isn't here. Who sits in a coffee shop all day?

But then the restroom door opens. And the guy comes out! He walks to the only empty table, pulls his laptop out of his backpack, settles down, and starts typing.

I want to go inside the coffee shop and sit with him. I want to ask what he's typing, get to know him, and maybe, let him get to know me. But it's too risky. I can't trust this guy. I can't trust anyone.

Suddenly, the guy glances up. I dart away from the window before he sees me—I hope—and start running again. I don't stop until I arrive at my motel room door, lungs burning. I rush inside, lock the door, and build my barricade with the table, chair, and nightstand. Then I pull off my sweat-soaked, dusty clothes. Naked, except for flip-flops, I step under the shower's warm spray.

And I breathe.

Chapter Four

I actually slept last night. Not just in fits of an hour or two at a time. I slept ten hours in a row.

I jump out of bed, eat, wash up, and get dressed in less than ten minutes. Then I burst out of my awful motel room and leave it behind as fast as I can, heading to the coffee shop. Today, I will sit and savor every drop of a nice cup of coffee, without crying. I'll even treat myself to a high-priced muffin. And then a thought hits me: *The guy who was there yesterday could be there again today.* That makes me anxious. But almost in a good way.

I arrive at the coffee shop and find it packed with people. The guy from yesterday *is* there, sitting at a table alone, typing on his laptop. My heart pounds. I don't allow my gaze to rest on him.

"The usual?" the girl behind the counter asks when I approach.

I'm surprised that she remembers me. "Yes," I say.

"And I'll also have a blueberry muffin."

"For here or to go?" she asks.

All of the chairs along the window are occupied, and there isn't even one empty table. "To go."

Seconds later, I have my muffin—in a small paper bag—and a coffee.

As I turn away from the counter, I hear a familiar voice. "You can sit here if you like." It's *him*. When my gaze meets his, he smiles. Although I don't trust them, his eyes intrigue me.

Without a word, I deposit my muffin on his table and take my coffee to the cream and sugar station. I feel safer looking at the guy from this distance. He's absorbed again with his laptop. His fingers move over the keyboard rapidly, almost like he's playing a musical instrument rather than typing words into a computer. His wavy, brown hair hides his eyes when he leans forward. His clothes are the kind most people would only wear around the house: dirt-brown pants that hang loosely over his long legs and a threadbare t-shirt. He's not attempting to impress anyone, and that impresses me.

I return to his table and quietly put down my coffee cup, trying not to disturb the guy. He doesn't seem to notice that I've joined him. *Good, he's not expecting a conversation.* I take a sip of my coffee and pop a piece of muffin into my mouth, squishing a large juicy blueberry with my tongue.

Suddenly, the guy closes his laptop. He stares at it for a moment, as if awakening from a trance, and then looks at me and says, without missing a beat, "Are you new to L.A.?"

I hastily swallow the food in my mouth. "Uh, yeah."

He seems to be expecting more. When I don't offer anything further he says, "I see."

"I'm visiting," I blurt out awkwardly.

"Cool. Where from?"

"New York."

He smiles as if I just mentioned his long-lost friend. "I was born there. In the city."

"Me too. But we moved out to Long Island before I started elementary school. You live in Los Angeles now?" *I can't believe I'm having a normal getting-to-know-you conversation with a stranger.*

"My family moved out here when I was three years old. How long are you visiting for?"

"I leave in four days. I'm supposed to start college in New York next week." I feel my shoulders tighten.

The guy looks down. "My college starts next week too."

"What's your major?"

"It was going to be pre-law, but I switched to creative writing."

"*You* were going to be a *lawyer*?" He doesn't look like the lawyer type. He's too artsy.

35

"Yeah, like my father. But I hate law. And when you get diagnosed with cancer, you get your priorities straight."

My gut twists. I hardly know this guy, but his revelation hits me hard. "You have cancer?" I ask gently.

"I did. Not anymore."

"That's good" is all I can think of to say.

The guy looks contemplative for a moment, and then he brightens. "So, why'd you come to L.A.? Business or pleasure?"

"Pleasure, I guess. At least I was hoping." And then I admit, "I kind of wanted to figure out if life was worth living."

The guy searches my face. I think he's waiting for me to laugh and say that I'm just kidding. But I don't. Finally, he says, "This is an unusually deep conversation considering that we haven't formally introduced ourselves."

"I'm Erin," I say, giving a small wave rather than offering my hand.

"I'm Ben," he says, waving back with a small smile.

As I gaze at him, I realize that, for the first time in a while, I'm letting someone look into my eyes without feeling afraid that they'll see what's there. I almost *want* Ben to see what's there. I want to know him. And I want him to know me. But, at the same time, the thought of Ben and me getting to know each other is terrifying.

"I have to go," I say, grabbing what's left of my muffin and coffee.

Ben's forehead furrows in confusion. "I hope to see you again."

I try to convince myself that it would be okay to stay here with Ben. To talk to him more. To *not* be afraid. But I can't. "I'm sorry that I have to go," I say honestly.

And then I leave.

* * *

It took only an hour for the public bus to get me all the way from Hollywood to Santa Monica. I step out of the icy air-conditioned bus into a warm breeze and start walking. Minutes later, I am standing where pavement meets sand, staring at the Pacific Ocean.

I remember coming here with Star, the two of us racing in the warm sand, heading toward the ocean. The memory of Star's laughter echoes in my head. I pull off my sneakers and socks and run, my feet sinking into the sun-drenched sand as I chase Star's giggles toward the water.

When I'm close to the families that dot the transition from dry sand to wet, I slow to a walk, looking for a place to set down my things. I finally lay my bag and sneakers a few feet from a crumbling sandcastle. A little boy who is digging out a moat around the castle dashes toward the ocean with an empty bucket, squealing. His mother acknowledges me with a hasty glance and then returns her attention to her phone.

I remove the t-shirt and shorts that cover my swimsuit,

pull my goggles down over my eyes, and start walking toward the ocean. The wet sand bubbles from the recent wave that kissed it. The sand is cold. The water must be colder. I don't hesitate though. I continue into the icy ocean. Every few moments, a wave hits my body. Higher and higher. I keep walking until a wave crashes over my head. When I swim out on the other side, my feet no longer reach the sand. The waves gently lift me as they come. I close my eyes and let my body sink down into the ocean, listening to the soothing underwater sound.

Something whips my face. I open my eyes.

It must have been kelp. There are strands of it everywhere.

I dive deep, kicking hard and swimming fast, imagining I'm a dolphin exploring the depths of the ocean, stopping only to come up for air. I shoot under a massive mound of kelp, flipping over onto my back to admire the snarled green tendrils.

Something catches my eye. I swim in for a closer look.

The kelp undulates with the waves. A large object remains tangled within it.

A person ... a woman ... no, a girl ...

IT'S STAR.

Her eyes are open and lifeless. Her face looks terrified, as if she is screaming a silent scream. I gasp, but there's no air to breathe, and so I suck in water. I need to find the surface, but the ocean is churning so much that I can barely see. Bubbles surround me. I'm not sure which way is up anymore. My brain is so swollen with fear that I can't think straight.

Something grabs me from behind and pulls me backward. I fight, but it won't let go. Maybe it's better not to fight it. Maybe I should let it take me. Then this would all be over.

It drags me down ... or up ... I'm not sure which.

And then I feel air against my lips. A woman is talking in my ear, but I can't figure out what she's saying. I cough uncontrollably, sucking in air between coughs. My body is pulled through the water until my feet hit sand.

"Can you walk?" the woman asks me.

I push her away before I vomit a stomachful of water into the surf.

"Are you having any pain?" she asks me.

I shake my head and take a few steps onto the shore. Then I collapse.

* * *

A crinkly blanket covers my body. Things drop onto the sand around me: people, packages. I keep my eyes closed. The sun is too bright.

A hand reaches under my blanket, grazing my shoulder. My heart pounds hard against my ribs as the hand slips under my swimsuit and presses against my skin. Fast electronic beeps speed up and slow down every time I take a shaky breath.

"She's tachy," a deep voice says.

A shadow passes over me. I open my eyes.

"How you feeling?" The man who is speaking wears a uniform and a badge. Even so, I feel an overwhelming need to escape.

"I'm fine." I pull the oxygen mask from my face and try to get up.

"Just relax," the man says touching my arm. His words echo in my brain, but in a different tone. In a different time. In a different voice. In *Barry's* voice.

"GET AWAY FROM ME!" I shove him hard and force myself upright.

"I'm just trying to help you," the uniformed man says, looking at me with concern. His badge says he's a paramedic. *He isn't going to hurt me. He is trying to protect me.*

"I'm sorry," I mumble.

A wave breaks with a thunderous clap. My eyes spring toward the ocean. Out in the water is a lifeguard—possibly the same woman who rescued me—swimming toward the shore. She's dragging something with her. A second lifeguard meets her with a blanket, just like the one on me. He quickly covers the thing with the blanket, but I catch a glimpse of it. *A person wrapped in kelp. The person I saw in the ocean.*

It can't possibly be Star. I know that in my head, but I

have to prove it to my heart. I pull off the wires attached to my chest and make my way to the lifeguards, astonished that I have the strength to walk. As I approach the female lifeguard, she moves in front of me, blocking my path.

"I need to see what's under that blanket," I say to her.

She shakes her head. Her short blond hair drips water onto her shoulders. "Sorry. No."

Tears form in my eyes. "When I was out there in the ocean, I saw a girl tangled up in the kelp. I need to know who she was."

The lifeguard presses her lips together and exhales. "We think she's the girl who got caught in a rip current off Venice Beach two days ago."

"I need to see her face," I say, my eyes fixed on the blanket.

"There are some things you just can't unsee, as much as you wish you could," she says.

I understand exactly what she means—more than she will ever know. "I *need* to see her. Please."

"How old are you?" she asks.

"Eighteen," I answer.

"I'm going to advise you not to," she says, then she takes a small step to the side. "But if you feel this is something you must do, I won't stop you."

I drop to my knees next to the blanket and lift one corner.

Chapter Five

The girl under the blanket doesn't look anything like Star. She doesn't even look real. Her face is bloated and purple. Her eyes are opaque. Her long brown hair is matted in knots. Her torn swimsuit has smiling cartoon flowers printed all over it. It is a stark reminder that this body once belonged to a living human being. It's hard to imagine that, just two days ago, this girl went for a swim in the ocean, and now her life is over.

I lower the blanket back to the sand. The lifeguard was right—the image of that girl will never leave my mind. It will join the other horrible things that have taken up residence there.

I go back to the lifeguard. "Thank you for letting me see her," I say.

"I hope it was the right thing to do." Her gaze searches my face, as if looking for the answer.

"It was," I assure her, but her forehead furrows with

uncertainty.

Before I leave I add, "And thank you for saving my life." But I'm not sure if I'm glad that she did.

The crowd of onlookers parts for me as I walk away in search of my belongings. I've been gone so long that the thought that someone might have taken my things, thinking they were abandoned, crosses my mind. But there really wasn't much to take, just some old clothes, cheap sunglasses, and a towel. My money is in a waterproof wallet still hung around my neck, and I left my phone and camera in the motel room.

I finally spot the little boy with the sandcastle. He's sailing a toy boat in the castle moat, oblivious to the dead girl lying on the sand about fifty feet away. I can tell by the look of unease on his mother's face that she is painfully aware of the girl.

"I saw the whole thing," the woman says to me in a hushed tone when I sit down on the sand next to my things. "You must have a guardian angel watching over you."

I nod as I wrap my towel around me.

The woman looks toward the blanket-covered body on the sand. "Is that the girl who drowned at Venice Beach the other day?"

"I don't know," I respond.

"Did you see the story about her on the news?" she persists.

I stare at the ocean. "No."

The woman types something into her phone and, after a few taps, hands it to me. On the screen is a photo of a girl with childlike eyes. Her long brown hair is pulled neatly back from her face. Words below the picture hit me like punches: "sixteen years old" "honor student" "wanted to be a doctor" "pushed her sister toward shore before she submerged." There's another photo below the story: the last photo taken of the girl. Her smile is carefree—the way mine was up until a few months ago. Her swimsuit is heart-wrenchingly familiar. Although the girl in the photo hardly resembles the body lying in the sand, I know now that they are the same person.

As I hand back the phone, I notice a man lugging a news camera, picking his way fast through the sand, heading toward the lifeguards.

"Looks like you're going to be famous!" the woman bursts out, as if it would be exciting to be on TV recounting what it was like to find a girl's dead body in the ocean.

"Not if I can help it." I yank my shirt and shorts over my damp bathing suit, stuff my towel and sneakers into my bag, and then I run.

* * *

I once heard that the easiest place to disappear is in a crowd, so I sprint toward Santa Monica Pier. During our trip to L.A., Star and I spent an afternoon there, enjoying the invigorating music, ocean views, and the omnipresent aroma of cotton candy. We bought veggie burgers, which we relished as we watched a vibrant, fiery sunset over the ocean. Then we took a twilight ride on the Ferris wheel.

Now, I weave myself into the suffocating throng of people on the pier. The sounds and smells that once made me feel exhilarated now overwhelm my senses: chattering voices, cooking meat, bells and dings, hip-hop music. I wish I could quiet all of it.

At the end of the pier, I duck inside the ladies room and rinse the lingering taste of vomit from my mouth. I feel weak and shaky. I should probably go try to eat something. I smooth my hair into a ponytail, put on my sunglasses, and head back outside.

Not far from the restroom is the place where Star and I bought our veggie burgers.

"Next," a man shouts from the window.

I hurry over to him. "A California veggie burger and a cup of ice water."

Moments later, I have a tray of food and no idea where to go. I don't want to sit at the tables, with all the people bustling around. And a sleeping man in ragged clothes occupies the bench where Star and I sat.

I walk until I'm behind a slatted fence, in an area that I'm sure isn't open to the public. It's not quiet here, but there's no one to talk to me or accidentally bump into me. I sit on a plastic crate, balance my tray in my lap, and take a bite of my burger. The seasoned veggies mix with the avocado and cheese and excite my taste buds. Memories of the last time I had this burger flood into me. Memories of a time when life seemed filled with infinite possibilities. A few months ago, all of those possibilities vanished in an instant. Tears fall down my face, but I don't bother wiping them away. I close my eyes and take bite after bite of my burger, until it's gone.

* * *

Angry waves crash onto the sand. Those waves could pull me into the ocean, but I won't let them. I stay far enough away that they can't touch me, and I walk fast, parallel to the shore.

The ocean is teeming with swimmers and surfers. Ahead of me, kids with boogie boards run from the beach and dive into the water, yelling to each other gleefully. Seeing small children play so fearlessly makes me feel ridiculous about being afraid of the ocean. Still, it's hard not to fear the ocean, now that I've seen what it can do.

By the time I turn around, Santa Monica Pier is far behind me and I am out of breath. I trudge up the beach, toward the T-shirt shops and beachside restaurants line the boardwalk. I pull on my sneakers and walk along the pavement, glancing up every intersecting street I encounter, trying to find one that looks familiar. Finally, I ask a woman whose sun-bleached hair makes me think that she might be a local, "Do you know how to get to the Venice

Canals?"

"Head up Venice Boulevard and look for the sign on the right," she says with a slight drawl.

A few intersections later, I turn up Venice Boulevard and feel a reassuring sense of déjà vu. Soon, I see the weathered sign that led Star and me into a hidden neighborhood of homes along picture-perfect waterways. I follow a small street until I see homey bungalows and skinny mansions lining broad canals. Their backyards and a narrow public walkway separate the houses from the water. Rowboats and kayaks are tied to miniature docks on the canal.

When we visited the canals, Star said that, if she lived in one of these homes, she would start every day by going kayaking. Many people say such things, but I had no doubt that Star would actually do it. Star was going to move to Los Angeles after she finished law school. She loved swimming and surfing as much as hiking, snowboarding, and skiing. She said that, from L.A., you could quickly drive to a perfect location to do any of that. It used to amaze me how well she had her life figured out.

A group of ducklings and their mother clatter onto the walkway ahead of me. I don't want to disturb them, and so I pause to admire a house covered in layer upon layer of blossoming vegetation. It looks like something out of a fairytale. Pink and purple flowers engulf the fence and grow up over the gate, partially hiding a mural of the canal.

The painting seems to be almost a mirror image of what's behind me, although the real-life homes are a bit different from the ones in the mural. One home has a different paint job. One home is an entirely different structure. I move the flowers to get a better look at the mural.

"Can I help you?" a man's voice says from the other side of the fence.

I shouldn't have touched the flowers. I'm about to let them fall back into place, but something stops me. On the just-uncovered part of the mural are two girls, one with brown, wavy hair and one with straight, blond hair. My skin tingles with recognition. "Your mural. It's beautiful. Did you paint it?"

The man stands. His hair is gray and wild. He looks about the same age as my father, but much less serious. "My mother painted it."

I point to the girls in the mural with a shaky hand. "Do you know who those girls are?"

He shrugs. "Just two teenagers she saw here one day."

"I think that ... one of those girls is me." I take a breath to steady my voice. "The other one is my best friend, Star."

"Not a chance." The man shakes his head dismissively. "My mom painted that mural more than twenty years ago."

I look back at the mural with new eyes. The brown-haired girl is taller than the blond one. Star is ... was ... much taller than me. And the brown-haired girl is wearing a dress. I hardly ever wear dresses. My heart sinks. "Sorry to bother you," I say.

"No worries," the man says as he settles back down, probably into a chair.

The ducks have waddled off the walkway, into the canal, but I turn away from the direction that I was headed. I don't want to explore here anymore.

* * *

From the soft sand of Venice Beach, I watch the ocean, half-expecting that it will leap up and engulf me at any moment. Honestly, it wouldn't surprise me right now if it did.

To say that my trip to L.A. hasn't gone as I'd hoped is an understatement. I had imagined that it would be reviving, inspiring, and most importantly, healing. I don't know why I thought L.A. would be able to heal me when everything else I've tried has failed. I guess that's what happens when people are desperate. They start to believe in miracles.

Far from shore, pelicans bob on the undulating water. Past them, a seabird dives into the ocean with a splash and disappears. Further away, a dolphin arches out of the water for an instant and then dives back down. Another dolphin appears just behind the first one, heading in the same direction. Moments later, the two surface side-by-side. And I realize what I've been missing. What I need if I am going to survive.

* * *

I can barely contain my energy on the bus ride back to Hollywood from Santa Monica. The bus drops me off just steps from my motel, but I rush past it, hardly acknowledging it with a glance. I dodge pedestrians on the busy sidewalks, and I race all the way to the coffee shop.

There are only a few people inside. Ben is among them, sitting by himself at the same table as he was this morning, typing on his laptop. My heart beats harder and faster. I go through the coffee shop door, march over to Ben's table, and sit down. I wait quietly until he looks up at me expectantly.

"Hi," I say.

"Hello," he says.

I take far too long to figure out what to say next, but Ben waits patiently, his expression open. Finally I ask, "What were you typing?"

"A script."

"What's it about?" I ask.

He shakes his head. "I don't know yet."

"What do you mean?"

He sighs. "I'm kind of lost."

"But you were typing so fast."

He turns his computer screen toward me. On it I see:

BOY

Hi.

GIRL

Hello.

BOY

Hi.

GIRL

Hello.

BOY

Hi.

GIRL

Hello.

BOY

Hi.

GIRL

Hello.

BOY

Hi.

GIRL

Hello.

BOY

Hi.

GIRL

Hello.

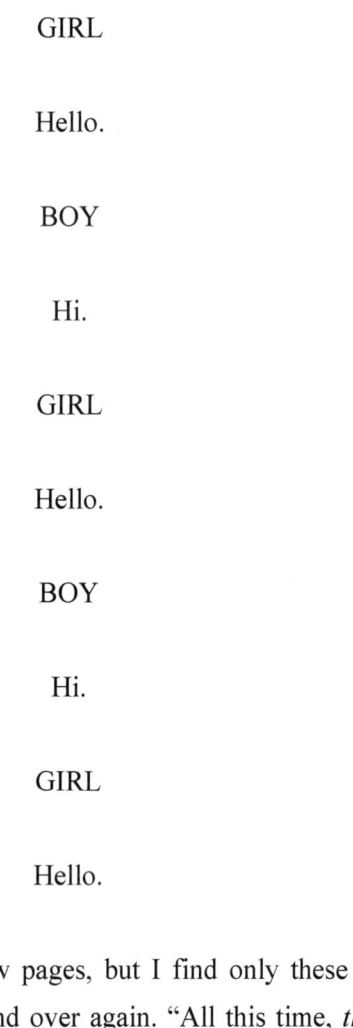

I scroll back a few pages, but I find only these four words, repeated over and over again. "All this time, *that's* what you've been typing?" I ask.

"Yup." Ben's gaze falls to the table. "I haven't even settled on the character's names yet."

"But I thought you *loved* writing."

"I do. And I have all these stories swimming around in my brain, but every time I try to start writing one of them … nothing. They say if you can't figure out what to write, then you should just write anything, and eventually the story will come. And so I keep typing, hoping something will happen."

"How long have you been at it?"

"Too long." Ben closes his laptop. "Enough about my writing. How was your day?"

"It was … well …" My eyes dampen. "It sucked."

Ben reaches toward my arm as if he's going to try a comforting touch.

Fear courses through me. *Don't touch me. Please don't touch me.*

He pulls back his hand and rests it on his thigh. "What happened?"

"I went for a swim at the beach and … I found a dead body in the water." The image of the girl's knotted hair and lifeless eyes surges into my mind. Ben looks at me with the same look that strangers have been giving me a lot lately, the look that makes me feel like they think I'm insane. "I'm not crazy," I say, harshly.

"I didn't think you were," Ben says.

"It was the girl who drowned two days ago at Venice Beach," I say. "Did you hear about her?"

"Yeah, I did," he says.

Maybe then he doesn't think I've lost my mind. I

continue, "When I saw her body, under the water, I freaked out. I was below this big mound of kelp, and I nearly drowned. A lifeguard found me. If she hadn't, I would have died."

Ben gives me a gentle smile. "I'm glad you didn't die."

"Me too," I whisper, and I almost mean it.

"You look like you could use some air," Ben says. "Want to take a walk?"

"With you?"

He laughs. "Well, yeah."

I should hesitate, but I don't.

Chapter Six

"But I was actually wearing *ladies pajamas*," Ben finishes.

I picture Ben standing on stage singing his heart out, wearing baby-blue silk pajamas. I laugh; I can't help myself. I have no doubt that, once Ben starts to write, his scripts will be pure gold. "Your stories are amazing!" I say.

"That wasn't a story. That really happened!" Ben protests, and then he admits, "The rest were stories though."

We stroll past a café where a waiter is lighting the candles on the tables, now that day is turning to night. My stomach grumbles.

"Are you hungry?" Ben asks me.

"A little," I say.

He races up the block so fast that I have to jog to keep up with him. He stops right in front of the restaurant that I wanted to eat at last night but avoided because I was alone. I'm not alone tonight. "Do you want to eat here?" he asks.

A smile spreads across my face. "I would love to."

As we enter the restaurant, a harried waitress, with a tray full of scrumptious-looking burgers piled with toppings, bowls exploding with fresh veggies drizzled with dressings, and paper cones stuffed with crispy fries, glances up. "Sit wherever you want. I'll be right there."

We step out onto the sidewalk patio. Unlike last night, it's fairly empty. About half of the tables are unoccupied. Ben chooses a corner table, tucked next to a tree speckled with tiny white lights. I pick up a menu and page through it. I'm so hungry that everything sounds good. It feels impossible to settle on what to order.

"What can I get you?" the waitress asks as she rushes up to our table.

"I'm good," Ben answers.

I'm still frantically looking through the menu, trying to make a decision.

"Should I give you a few minutes?" the waitress sighs.

"No." I quickly choose. "A vegetarian Cobb salad … And fries."

She makes a note on her pad. "Anything to drink?" she asks without looking up.

"Ice water."

"Great," she snaps before she stalks off.

"Bit of an attitude, don't you think?" Ben whispers as soon as the waitress is back inside the restaurant.

"She's probably busy," I say.

Ben smiles. "I like that about you."

"You like what?"

"You give people the benefit of the doubt."

I look at him with narrowed eyes. "Wait ... so when you said, 'Bit of an attitude, don't you think?' you were leading the witness?"

Ben shrugs. "Maybe."

"You were trying to get me to say, 'Yeah, she's a real—'"

"And it didn't work. See, I would have been an awful lawyer."

"If you *wanted* to be a lawyer, you'd be a good one."

"I *want* to be a writer, and I'm not very good at that." There is pain in his voice. Ben stares down at the white tablecloth as if he's dissecting it with his eyes. It's the kind of thing I would do if I was trying not to cry, but I don't think Ben is on the verge of tears. Still, he looks miserable.

I wish I could make his sadness go away, like he's done with mine for the past few hours. "Maybe you're trying too hard. Maybe you should take a break. You could hang out with me tomorrow." I immediately wonder if that isn't such a good idea. I hardly know this guy.

Before I can change my mind, Ben says, "All right."

* * *

Ben insisted on walking me back to my motel. Part of me is glad he did because there were some scary-looking men who were eyeing me on the way.

"We're here," I say as the motel comes into view. I immediately feel embarrassed by the place. I don't want Ben to get a closer look at it. "I'm good now. Thanks for walking me here."

"I should get you to your door," Ben offers.

I don't want Ben to come to my door. *What if he tries to come in?* "I'll be fine."

"Okay," he says. "See you tomorrow at eight?"

We agreed to meet at the coffee shop tomorrow morning to start our day together.

"Yeah, I'll see you then." I start walking away.

When I am halfway to my motel room door, I turn back and see Ben still standing where I left him. He hasn't moved at all.

"What are you waiting for?" I call out.

"I'm waiting until you're inside," he says matter-of-factly.

I turn around and keep walking. I didn't want Ben to know which room I'm in, but I think him watching me get there *is* probably a good idea.

I push the key into the lock of my motel room door. It won't turn. I jiggle it and try again.

A gruff male voice groans from inside the room and then shouts, "Go away!"

I jump away from the door in shock.

"What's wrong?" Ben yells out.

Instinctually, I head toward him. He meets me

halfway.

"There's a man in my room!" I whisper to him.

"Are you sure you had the right room?" Ben asks.

And then my stomach drops. I turn and run toward the motel office.

"Where are you going?" Ben calls after me.

"I forgot to pay today," I say, breathing hard, from panic rather than physical exertion.

"Don't they just charge your credit card?" Ben asks as he catches up with me.

"I'm paying cash. I have to pay every morning."

I collide with the office door and shove it open. Ben follows me inside.

The man at the desk looks up with a vacant gaze—different from the other times that I've seen him. The open bottle of liquor next to him tells me that he's probably been drinking. "Can I help you?" he asks.

"Where's my stuff?" I shout at him, my heart pounding.

"Calm down." He points to some black trash bags behind the counter. "It's all right here."

I take a breath, ever-so-slightly relieved. "So I forget to pay for one day and you go into my room, take out my things, and change the lock?"

"Actually, it's *my* room. You were just renting it ... 'til you stopped paying," he says. "By the way, I deducted twenty-five dollars from your deposit to pay for changing the lock."

I am livid, but the mistake was mine, and so I am at his mercy. "So now what am I supposed to do?"

"If you pay for the night, I can put you in another room," he offers with a pointy smile that chills my blood.

"I want my stuff first," I say. The truth is, I don't have enough money in my waterproof wallet to pay him. I left most of my cash inside my luggage, along with my camera and phone.

The man drops my suitcase and the trash bags on my side of the counter. My heartbeat rises to my throat when I don't find my camera and phone where I left them. I dig around in the suitcase and finally find them in a completely different spot—zipped into a compartment where I never would have put them. It makes my stomach turn to think that this man pawed through my things, even if he didn't take anything.

Ben kneels down next to me. "You don't have to stay here," he says.

I stare at my violated belongings. "I can't afford anyplace else."

Without a pause, Ben says, "Come stay with me."

Although it's a completely absurd idea, part of me wants to grab my things and leave with Ben. His place has to be better than this. And, for some reason, I feel safe with Ben. But feeling safe with a man is dangerous. If I go with Ben, he'll probably expect something, something I can't afford to give. "I'm fine," I say without looking at him. "Thanks."

I find my cash exactly where I hid it. I remove 50 dollars and pay the man at the desk.

"Room Twenty-nine," he says. "Same key."

I dump the contents of the trash bags into my suitcase, except for the flip-flops—which I pinch together between two fingers, their certainly-germ-laden soles touching.

"Have a good night!" the man calls out as Ben and I leave the office. It sounds like more of a taunt than a pleasantry.

A sign near the rusted vending machine indicates that Rooms 20 through 30 are located at the back of the property, and so we turn down the dingy, isolated alleyway that leads there. Room 29 is the second-to-last room in the row. All of the porch lights nearby are either burned out, smashed, or missing. I'm glad Ben is with me.

I turn my key in the lock, and the door clicks open. The smell of urine mixed with beer permeates the stale air inside the room. When I flip the light switch, at least ten shiny brown insects run across the floor and disappear under the bed.

"Were those cockroaches?" I ask Ben, swallowing my disgust.

"I think so," Ben says, sounding equally disgusted.

I step forward, resigning myself to the fact that I will sleep here tonight.

I'm about to set my suitcase on the battered table when Ben steps in front of me. "Erin, you deserve better than this," he says, staring into my eyes. "I'll help you find another place."

I shake my head. "I told you, I can't afford—"

"I'll cover the difference."

"I can't take your money, Ben."

"Then come stay with me."

I look away from him, because I can't look at him and say what I'm about to say. "I'm not going to have sex with you."

"Is that what you think I want?" Ben asks.

I stare at the soiled carpet beneath my feet. "If I go back to your place, that's what you're going to expect."

"Number one: It's not my place; it's my mom's. And number two: I don't want *anything* in return."

Ben seems to care about me. But why should he? He hardly knows me. And I hardly know him. I shouldn't trust him. So why do I feel like I should?

And then he adds in a whisper, "I know someone hurt you."

My breath catches in my chest. *How could he know that? Am I so damaged that it's obvious?* Shame gives way to anger. It surges through my nerves, burning my flesh. *Yes, someone hurt me. Lots of people, actually.* But I will *never* be a victim again. I will not let *anyone* take advantage of me. Not Ben. Not that creepy man at the front desk. Not anyone. Even if I *die* trying to stop them.

I hurl my flip-flops into the trashcan and storm out the door, propelled by a pure rage.

"Where are you going?" Ben asks, running after me.

"I'm going to get my money back."

* * *

The man who accepted my money just minutes ago now appears to be asleep in his chair behind the counter in the motel office. I slam my room key down in front of him. The man opens his eyes instantly. I doubt he was actually sleeping.

"Checking out!" I shout.

He barely hides his smirk. "But you already paid for the night."

"That room is unacceptable," I say, my voice strong and firm.

"What's wrong with it?" he asks, feigning concern.

"It smells like urine. And there are cockroaches in there."

He raises his thick eyebrows. "Little girl, at the rate you're paying, that room is a gift."

"Well, I'm not staying there, so give me my money back."

He sighs and grabs a rusty aerosol can. "I'll go spray it down for ya, make it smell nice."

"No, I've had enough. I want my money back." My

legs are trembling. I'm glad the man can't see them from behind the counter.

His gaze hardens. "I need to inspect the room first. For all I know, you trashed it."

My hands ball into fists, my fingernails cutting into my palms. "Are you *kidding* me?"

The man comes out from behind the counter. He walks right up to me and stands too close. "No." His breath stinks of cigarettes and alcohol. "I'm *dead* serious." He looks my body up and down, and then he sneers. "Are you coming with me?" he asks.

I feel the blood drain from my face. "We'll wait here."

The man stares at me for full minute with dead eyes before he grumbles, "Wait outside."

He follows Ben and me out of the office and locks the door behind us. As soon as he disappears around the corner, Ben says, "We should go."

"But I need to get my money back," I say.

"How much does he have?" Ben asks.

"One hundred fifty dollars. Wait, no, he subtracted twenty-five dollars from the deposit to change the lock. One hundred twenty-five dollars."

"It isn't worth it. He might come back here with a knife or a gun." Ben's eyes plead with mine.

Guilt hits me. Ben doesn't belong here. I don't want to put him in danger. "You should go. I'll meet you at the coffee shop in the morning."

He shakes his head. "I'm not going to leave you here."

"Why do you even care? You don't know me." My voice sounds accusatory even though I don't mean it to.

"I *want* to know you," Ben says.

And I believe him. I believe Ben cares. I trust him, even though I know I should trust no one. Before I can respond, the man comes back around the corner. I don't see any weapons with him, but that doesn't mean he doesn't have any. And even without weapons, he can still hurt us. He eyes me as he opens the office. Dismissing the warnings blaring in my brain, I follow him inside. Ben is right behind me.

"Are we done?" I ask the man, trying to sound impatient rather than scared.

"The room isn't as I left it—" he starts.

Anger swells inside me. I feel like I'm about to explode.

"That's enough!" Ben exclaims.

"Ben, I've got this," I say through clenched teeth. I turn to the man and say in a low voice, "You like taking advantage of people, don't you? It makes you feel like a big man, doesn't it? Well, you're NOT taking advantage of me." I smash my fist against the counter. A cup of pens and a display of brochures crash to the ground with a hollow sound. "PUT MY MONEY ON THE COUNTER, NOW!"

Ben moves closer to me. "Just give her money back and we'll go away."

"Don't worry, Ben," I say with absolute confidence. "He will." I stare at the man, unblinking, and growl, "I SAID, 'NOW!'"

Without breaking eye contact, the man reaches into his pocket, pulls out a few bills, and lays them on the counter. I count the money. *One hundred twenty-five dollars.* I stuff the cash into my pocket.

"Psycho bitch," the man says under his breath.

"*What* did you say?" Ben asks, approaching the desk.

"Don't bother, Ben," I say. "He's not worth it."

I grab my suitcase, and Ben and I back out of the office.

Neither of us says anything more until we are a few blocks north of the motel. Ben is the first to speak. "Where are we heading?" he asks.

"Your mom's house." I made that choice back when I hurled my flip-flops into the trash. It seemed like a better decision then, with all that anger pumping through me, than it does now. I should probably reconsider, but I don't have many options. It's dark and late, the streets are devoid of all but the most unpleasant-looking of people, and the cold night air is starting to pass right through the sweater I pulled from my suitcase.

"All right," Ben says flatly.

We walk in silence again, Ben leading me past the coffee shop where we met and the café where we ate dinner, and then toward Griffith Park, where the environs transition into a sleepy neighborhood of twisting roads lined with tall trees and gorgeous mansions.

"Are you mad at me?" I finally ask.

He shakes his head. "No."

But I'm unconvinced. "I'm sorry I put you in danger back there."

"Well, if I ever figure out how to write, someday it will make a great story," Ben says with a tired grin.

I imagine the story as Ben would tell it. "I bet that jerk will think twice before he messes with a 'little girl' again."

"I have to admit, I didn't think you had it in you." Ben glances into my eyes, and I feel a spark, like electricity. It must be what's left of the adrenaline.

I smile. "Me neither."

Ben's expression darkens. "Makes me wonder what else you're hiding."

My stomach flips uncomfortably. "You think I'm hiding something?"

"I think you have secrets."

"Doesn't everybody? I bet *you* have secrets."

"Yeah, I do," Ben says.

It makes me nervous how quickly he admitted to that. "What are your secrets?" I ask, unsure whether I want to hear the answer.

"What are yours?" he responds.

As much as I should want to know all of Ben's secrets before I follow him to wherever he's leading me, I'm not ready to tell him mine. "Just don't hurt me," I say. I'm not sure whether it's a threat or a plea.

"I wish I could promise you that, Erin," Ben says.

Fear chills my skin. "What is that supposed to mean?"

"Sometimes people hurt other people without trying to." Ben stops at the end of a meandering brick walkway that leads to an enormous, two-story, Spanish-style home surrounded by a perfectly-maintained garden of cacti. He starts up the path and then turns around and smiles, as if our conversation about secrets never happened. "Are you coming?"

My feet stay planted. "Shouldn't you let your mom know first?"

"My mom is in Paris on vacation."

My stomach tightens. "When you said we were going to your mom's house, I thought she'd be here."

"Well, she's not," he says. "Is that okay?"

I could leave now. Maybe I should. But where would I go?

I won't let Ben take advantage of me. I won't let him hurt me.

"Yeah," I say. "That's okay."

My heart pounding, I follow Ben to the side door of the house.

"We have a spare key in the squirrel statue," Ben says. "You can hold onto it while you're here."

I pick up the ceramic squirrel and remove the key from

the compartment in the bottom.

"The lock sticks a little," Ben continues. "Go ahead and try it out."

I have to work the key to get it into the lock, but then the door pops open. I step into a darkened room—a kitchen. A wiry, black-and-white cat, wearing a jingle-bell collar, darts into the room to greet us.

"That's Bolt," Ben introduces the cat.

I lean down and pet Bolt as he purrs affectionately. Bolt follows us down a hallway lined with photos of far-away places: London Bridge, the Eiffel Tower, a gondola floating in the water under a white bridge, cherry-blossom trees with a white-capped mountain in the background. We pass a boy's bedroom with its dark-blue walls speckled with tiny white stars and a model of the solar system hanging from the ceiling. It reminds me a bit of Star's bedroom. Ben hunches his shoulders like an embarrassed child. "That's my room. I keep wanting to update the décor, but I think my mom likes that it's the way it was when I was a kid."

"I think astronomy is cool," I say.

His eyes brighten. "If you want, I can take you to Griffith Observatory."

"Yeah, maybe." I don't know if I'm ready to go back to the place where, just yesterday, I couldn't help imagining myself jumping to my death.

Ben leads me into an immaculate room. Pinks, greens,

and floral prints welcome me, along with the scent of peaches—likely from the crystal bowl of potpourri on the nightstand. The bed is covered with a canopy. It's the princess bed that I always wanted when I was a little girl.

"This is our guest room. Sorry, it's a little *pink*," Ben says.

I smile. "It's wonderful."

"There are clean towels in the guest bathroom. Do you need anything else?"

"No," I say. "Thank you, Ben."

He stands there, looking at me, his expression unreadable. I'm not sure what he's waiting for, but he doesn't wait long. "Goodnight then."

"Goodnight."

Ben leaves the room, followed by Bolt, and I quietly shut the door behind them. There is no lock. I consider for a moment wedging the nightstand and desk against the door to form a barricade, but everything in my being tells me that I can trust Ben. And so, instead of a building a barricade, I lodge a mouse-shaped squeaky cat toy under the door. That way I'll know if Ben opens the door while I'm asleep. But somewhere deep inside me, I feel certain that he won't.

I close my eyes and take a deep breath of the peach-scented air.

For the first time since I arrived in L.A., I feel safe.

Chapter Seven

A pillow slams down over my face. Hands press it forcefully, angrily against my mouth. Panic fills my chest. *I can't breathe.* I struggle to push the pillow away, but it won't budge. I try desperately to suck in air, but I can't get enough.

Something hits the pillow, sending a sting through my nose, again and again. I claw and kick, desperately fighting for my life, but the harder I fight, the weaker I get. My air is running out, taking my strength along with it. My arms and legs grow useless. I want to keep fighting, but I can't. My body has unwillingly surrendered.

The pillow lifts from my face. I gasp air I never thought I'd breathe again, feeling life return to me. But I don't dare open my eyes. *If I pretend to be unconscious, maybe he'll leave me alone.*

Suddenly, hands grab my hips, scratching my skin with their fingernails. My panties slip down past my knees, and weight falls on top of me. My legs are pushed apart. I bite my lip to silence a scream. I try not to feel his thighs against mine. I try not to hear his grunts and moans as he forces himself into me. I try to make myself numb, but it's impossible to ignore the stabbing pain that's slicing through me. It hurts so much … all the way down to my soul.

I inhale the sweet smell of peaches.

Why does it smell like peaches?

My eyelids pop open.

I am all alone. In Ben's guest room. The door is closed and the mouse-shaped cat toy is still wedged right up against it. The pain I just experienced was a memory. A memory of my night with Barry. A night that will haunt me as long as I live.

I slip out from under the covers, move the cat toy, and open the door. Bolt comes running to greet me, his bell jingling. I pet his silky fur for a minute while he purrs, then I follow the sound of a TV to the kitchen. My heart speeds when I see Ben sitting at the kitchen table, sipping a cup of tea.

"Good morning!" he says as if it's the most normal thing in the world to have a virtual stranger walk into his mom's kitchen first thing in the morning. Then again, considering how easily he invited me here, maybe for Ben it is.

I take a breath, searching for strength. "Good morning," I answer.

"Help yourself to whatever's in the cabinet and the fridge," Ben offers.

After a brief forage, I grab a jar of almond butter and bag of granola, along with a glass of water, a bowl, and a spoon, and I join Ben at the table. On the TV, a meteorologist is reviewing the forecast. His graphic shows seven days of bright-yellow suns.

"Does it ever rain here?" I ask, pouring some granola into the bowl.

"Occasionally. Mostly in the winter."

"It rains all the time in New York." I like the rain. It makes the indoors feel warm and secure, and it makes the outdoors smell like clean dirt. I spoon some almond butter onto the granola and dig in.

Ben looks at my breakfast, amused. "So, what's on tap for today?"

I want to take a break from memories. I want to do something that Star and I had planned to do, but didn't get around to. "I was thinking about going to see the stars in the sidewalk along Hollywood Boulevard and the celebrity hand and footprints—" My attention is suddenly captured by a photo that flashes up on the TV screen and turns my skin cold. It's a picture of a carefree girl wearing a swimsuit patterned with smiley-faced flowers. "That's the girl from the ocean," I breathe.

The reporter continues, "The sixteen-year-old's body was discovered by a swimmer yesterday morning, just off the beach in Santa Monica."

"The swimmer was you?" Ben asks.

I nod.

The reporter goes on, "Funeral services will be held for Alexis Reynolds at Saint Charles Borromeo Church tomorrow afternoon at five. Members of the public are invited to attend."

"You should go to the funeral," Ben says.

I push my almond-butter-coated spoon into the granola, no longer hungry. "But I didn't know her."

"You kind of met."

I shake my head. "I hate funerals. I didn't even go to my best friend's."

Ben's eyes narrow. "Your best friend died?"

"Yeah," I say.

"What did they die of?" he asks.

I take a sip of my water, fighting the urge to cry. "I don't want to talk about it, okay?"

"Okay," Ben says. And then he adds, "You should think about going to Alexis's funeral though. It might give you some closure."

"I'll think about it," I say. And I will.

But I won't go.

* * *

A man in a tattered superhero costume wanders past Ben and me as we walk along a sidewalk adorned with brass-and-stone stars. The back of the man's outfit has been carelessly repaired with duct tape. Ahead of us, a disheveled woman in grimy clothes leans against a wall, talking loudly with someone who isn't there.

I turn to Ben. "This place makes me sad." It's the same sense of despair that I've felt in other cities, even in other parts of Los Angeles, but here on Hollywood Boulevard, with reminders of so many dreams come true stuck into the sidewalk, it's even more disheartening.

"Maybe you'll like the celebrity hand and footprints better. They're over there," Ben says, pointing just ahead.

He leads me into a courtyard where tourists mill around snapping photos of the ground. I half-heartedly look down at the hand and shoeprints and the autographs preserved in cement.

"Hey!" Ben calls out. "My feet are the same size as Indiana Jones'!" He's standing in Harrison Ford's footprints, smiling so broadly that he looks goofy.

His unbridled enthusiasm makes me smile. "How about your hands?"

Ben reaches down. His fingers extend far beyond those in Ford's handprints.

"I hadn't noticed this before, but you have freakishly-big hands!" I tease.

"You know what they say about big hands, don't

you?" Ben asks.

Is he making some kind of crude reference? "No," I say, guarded.

"Big hands, big heart." He shifts his gaze to the ground. "Whose footprints do you fit in?"

"Wait a second. I want to get a photo of you there," I say, pulling out my camera. Ben puts on an even bigger grin and I snap a picture. It's the first photo I've taken since I arrived in Los Angeles.

I tuck my camera into my pocket and look for an actress's footprints to try to fit my sneakers into. Many of the women were wearing heels when their footprints were preserved so it's hard to tell if our feet are the same size. I finally find an exact match with one of my favorite actresses. "My feet are the same size as Meryl Streep's," I shout out to Ben.

Ben jogs over. "Cool. Let's get a picture."

I hold out my camera to a fellow tourist and ask him, "Would you mind taking a picture of us?"

Ben moves closer to me. With our bodies just centimeters apart, I feel the energy between us pulling us together. I take a shaky breath.

The man aims the camera and says, "*Ichi, ni, san.*" He snaps a photo and hands the camera back.

"*Domo arigato gozaimasu,*" Ben says to him.

I nod my head in agreement, assuming, based on the man's polite bow, that Ben said something nice. "What did you say to him?" I ask Ben, as we walk away.

"'Thank you very much' in Japanese," he answers.

"You speak Japanese?"

"My mom taught me a bunch of languages when I was a kid. She told me that learning different languages is like traveling the world without leaving home."

"Does she travel a lot?" I ask.

"No, her trip to Paris is her first one outside of the United States." Ben sighs. "I wish I could have gone with her."

"I'm sure you'll get the chance someday." I imagine myself in Paris with Ben, walking down the narrow cobblestone streets I've seen in movies. As we pass boutiques, cafés, and bakeries with French names, Ben does something I could never handle in real life: he puts his arm around me. In my imagination, I rest my head on his shoulder, feeling completely content. I shake off the daydream and tuck my camera back into my pocket. "I guess I've seen enough of this place."

"You sound disappointed," Ben notes.

"It just wasn't what I was expecting to find here."

"I want to show you something," Ben says.

"What?" I ask.

"It's a surprise," he says.

"I don't like surprises …" *anymore.*

"Do you trust me?" Ben offers his hand.

I stare at his hand, but don't accept it. "I want to."

77

"Good enough." He turns and starts walking away.

I follow him back along the sidewalk of Hollywood Boulevard. He stops in front of an ordinary-looking movie theater box office.

"You want to see a movie?" I ask, puzzled.

"Sort of." He takes out his wallet and checks the movie listings. "Let's go see … *Kid Docs*."

"It's on me," I say. It's the least I can do to try to repay Ben for letting me stay with him. I slide forty dollars to the woman on the other side of the glass. "Two adults for *Kid Docs*."

She hands me the tickets and my change. I stuff the money into my wallet and follow Ben toward a theatre that looms at the far end of the courtyard where we saw the hand and footprints. I pass Ben his ticket, but reflexively jerk my hand back at the last second so that we don't touch. The ticket slips out of Ben's fingers and lands in a footprint.

I look away as Ben scoops the ticket off the ground. "Sorry," I mumble.

"Why'd you pull away like that?" Ben asks, looking inquisitive rather than annoyed.

I don't look at him. "It wasn't personal."

"What was it then?"

I consider what he said last night. "You already think you know, don't you?"

"Someone hurt you?"

"Yeah, someone hurt me." *I wonder if it was smart to admit that to Ben.*

"If you want to talk about it—" Ben starts.

"I don't."

"So you're just going to go through the rest of your life without trusting anyone?"

My heart pounds, suddenly angry. "Why shouldn't I?"

"Because that's a sucky way to live."

"You have no idea what I went through. What I'm *still* going through."

"You're right, I don't. But I know what it's like to be betrayed."

Ben was betrayed? My eyes search his face. For an instant, it looks hopeless, like mine does when I stare into the mirror lately. Maybe he *does* understand what I'm going through. Not exactly, but enough.

"We're going to be late." Ben starts walking toward one of the three golden doors flanked by columns encircled with menacing spiked metal masks.

I run to catch up with him, my mind reeling. I want to ask him to tell me more, but instead I ask, "So what's this movie about?"

"I don't know."

"Then why did you want to see it?" I ask.

Before Ben answers, I step into the theater entryway, and I gasp. Aside from the glowing, modern concession stand straight ahead of us, we could be in the reception area of an elegant hotel half a world away. The dark walls are adorned with elaborate painted images of ancient China. An intricate, lantern-like chandelier hangs above us. The crimson carpet features the image of a dragon. "This place is amazing!" I breathe.

Ben smiles. "They use it for movie premieres."

We descend into an atmospheric auditorium that is a grander version of the lobby. Reds, browns, and golds cover the fantastic walls. There must be at least a hundred people occupying the seats, but the theater feels nearly empty. I sink into a plush velvet seat, as a scarlet curtain decorated with golden palm trees begins to part, revealing a tremendous movie screen.

Ben plops down in a seat next to me. "Is this anything like what you were hoping to find here?" he whispers.

I look into Ben's eyes, feeling like I might be able trust him wholly and completely ... not yet ... but maybe someday. "It's a hundred times better."

* * *

"That was one of the coolest things ever!" I say to Ben, as we leave the most magnificent movie theatre I ever been too.

"What movie did you see?" a woman who had been admiring the footprints in the courtyard asks me in a pretty accent that I can't place.

"*Kid Docs*, and it was amazing, but the theater was

incredible. It's gorgeous inside! There are fantastic murals and art. And the seats are covered in red velvet."

"That sounds wonderful!" She leans over to the woman next to her. "We should see a movie at the theatre here."

"How about tomorrow after we hike to the Hollywood Sign?" the other woman replies, in the same accent as the first woman.

"You can *hike* to the Hollywood Sign?" I ask her.

"There's a trail that takes you just above it," she answers.

"I could use a hike," Ben says.

The woman takes out her phone, pulls up a map, and shows me exactly how to get there. The trailhead is not too far from a stop of the same train that Ben and I took to get here. Before she puts her phone away, she asks me, "Would you mind taking a photo of us?"

I accept her phone. "No problem."

The women pose with one of the fanciful stone creatures by the theater entrance and mug for the camera. *Just like Star and I used to do.*

"That was cute," I say, feeling an ache of sadness in my gut.

"Do you want me to take a photo for you?" the woman with the phone offers.

"Sure."

I trade my camera for her phone and gesture to Ben to

come be in the picture. He moves closer to me, but I can tell he's being careful not to touch me. Even though I appreciate his consideration of my feelings, it hurts my heart.

"Smile!" the woman calls out as she aims the camera.

I smile, but my heart isn't into it. Without even looking at him, I can tell that Ben's isn't either.

***

"I'm sorry about what I said earlier," Ben says, as we walk past yet another one of the little bungalows that fit, like pieces of a giant jigsaw puzzle, onto the base of the mountain that sports the Hollywood Sign.

"What you said about what?" I ask.

"About you not trusting people," he says. "I shouldn't expect you to trust me."

"Good, because I don't," I say a little too harshly. I soften my voice. "I just ... I can't."

Ben drops his gaze to the ground. His hair falls in his face the way it does when he types on his laptop. "May I tell you another story?"

"What's it about?" I ask.

"It's *my* story."

I shiver. "Okay." So far, I've loved Ben's stories, but I get the feeling I won't like this one.

We walk along the winding road for a while before he speaks again, "I had an okay childhood. Not great, but okay. When I was twelve years old, things began to change. My father started beating me, sometimes until I was swollen and bloody. He usually left my face, arms, and legs alone though, so other people wouldn't see the bruises." As he speaks, Ben's voice is steady and unaffected, as if he's talking about the weather rather than the cruel beating of a helpless boy.

Ben continues, "I told myself that I would finally escape from my father when I went off to college, but when it came time to apply, he insisted on choosing the school and the classes. He decided that I would live at home and commute to campus. That's when I realized that he was going to find some way to control me for the rest of his life. I felt trapped."

Ben pauses for a deep breath. I take one too and hold it as he continues, "My father had a samurai sword that he was exceptionally proud of—he bought it during a trip to Japan. It hung on the wall of his office in downtown Los Angeles. One morning, I woke up early, rode the Metro to his office, took the sword off the wall, and stabbed myself in the chest with it. Over and over. Until I passed out.

"I woke up in the hospital," Ben goes on, his voice weaker now. "I had tubes coming out of places that should never have tubes in them. The doctors had cut open my ribcage and done surgery to stop the bleeding. Even with all of the painkillers flowing into my IV, it the worst physical pain I'd ever experienced.

"A psychiatrist and a social worker came to talk to me. They asked about all the old, healed scars on my body, and I told them about my father. They promised they would make the abuse stop. Then they brought my mom in, along with another doctor—an oncologist—and they told me I had cancer; the ER doctors had discovered it when they did the blood tests they do on trauma patients. A few days later, I began chemo. And my entire life got better. My mom and I started talking to a psychologist. My father moved out. I finally felt like my life had hope …"

I probably should say something, but everything I formulate in my mind feels wrong. I look over and see that Ben is distracted by a nearby sign.

"Horseback tours in the Hollywood Hills!" he reads. He points to the dusty dirt road up ahead. "The ranch is right at the end of this road! You want to go for a horseback ride?"

I don't, but Ben sounds so thrilled with the idea that I say, "Sounds great!"

He takes off running, and I race after him. He stops outside a large horse enclosure, breathless. I nearly collide with him, breathless as well.

"Have you ridden a horse before?" Ben asks me as he stares at the horses.

I swallow. The horses look much taller and more threatening up close than I thought they would. "No. Have you?"

"I used to ride all the time when I was a kid. But I haven't been on a horse since I was eight."

"Why not?" I ask.

"I'll tell you later."

Ben continues into the ranch. I take a deep breath and follow him.

Chapter Eight

For some reason, the horse I was assigned to ride prefers to walk on the outermost edge of the dirt trail, where one misstep would send us plunging down a steep mountainside that is covered in prickly shrubs.

Ahead of me—also on horseback—are three tourists from China, our guide, and Ben. We all wear ugly yellow plastic helmets, except for our guide, who wears a cowboy hat. Ben appears so relaxed that he looks like a real cowboy. *Even in his dorky helmet, he looks attractive.* I cringe. I can't let myself think of Ben like that. It's too dangerous.

My horse picks up her pace and moves past Ben's. I'm not sure whether it's safe to try slowing her down, so I don't. Now I can't see Ben unless I turn around, something I don't dare do on a horse. I wish I could see Ben. Seeing him in front of me was exactly what I needed to keep myself from freaking out. Now, panic rises in my chest. My heart pounds. My hands sweat so much that I'm not sure how I'll be able to hold on.

"You don't look like you're having fun," Ben calls out from behind me.

"I'm just ... nervous," I mutter.

Ben increases the speed of his horse to match mine. "Want some advice?"

"Okay," I say, feeling calmer with Ben by my side.

"When it comes to horses like these, if you let them, they'll take you exactly where you need to go. You need to trust the horse."

"I don't trust anyone or anything," I say. "How am I supposed to trust the horse?"

Ben doesn't get the chance to respond, because my horse increases her pace again, moving ahead of his. She seems to be sensing my fear, trying to escape it. I close my eyes and take a deep breath, willing myself to calm down. *One Mississippi, Two Mississippi, Three Mississippi. Three Mississippi, Two Mississippi, One Mississippi.* I try to relax my shoulders and arms, while still keeping a tight grip on the saddle. I feel myself shift a little. My heart heaves in my chest. I open my eyes and adjust my position.

I take another slow breath, this time keeping my eyes open. I relax my thighs, letting them rest against the horse's sides. *One Mississippi, Two Mississippi, Three Mississippi. Three Mississippi, Two Mississippi, One Mississippi.* And then, something changes. The horse and I begin to move together. Like we are one animal. Skinny tree branches sway in the breeze. The cowboy hat on our guide gently bobs up and down. I spot Griffith Observatory sitting regally on a cliff in the distance. In the opposite direction, glimmers of light reflect off the Pacific Ocean. Everything is so ... beautiful.

Unhurried hoofbeats approach me, almost matching the slow beat of my heart. And then Ben appears by my side again. He doesn't say anything and neither do I. I just take a calm breath, and I smile.

* * *

Ben and I—and our horses—are the last ones to arrive at the top of Mount Hollywood. The view here must be one of the most spectacular in all of Los Angeles: 360-degrees of mountains that give way to sprawling cities with clusters of skyscrapers. My horse parks herself next to Ben's, facing Mount Lee, where the Hollywood Sign resides.

Ben gives a half-smile that reveals a dimple in his right cheek. I like Ben. I really like him. I want to connect with him, but there's something stopping me. The problem is, I'm not sure if what's stopping me is my fear of trusting *anyone*, or whether there's something specific about *Ben* that I'm sensing, a warning sign I need to heed.

I look toward the Hollywood Sign, imagining what it will be like to be there with Ben. All alone. No horses. No other people. Just us. I picture Ben and me standing above the Hollywood Sign letters. Wind caresses my face. My hair whips up romantically behind me. Ben stands closer than should be comfortable for me, but I don't step away. He looks into my eyes as if he can see my soul, and I feel like I can see his; it is kind and good.

I take his hand and pull him toward me. I close my eyes, and Ben's lips press lightly against mine, parting just a little, making me warm and tingly all over. His hands glide down my back, holding me against him. I wait for the moment when his touch will change from tender to violent, but it doesn't come. He just holds me. And kisses me. Gently.

I pull away and look into his eyes again, studying them. I trust them. I trust him. I lift my shirt up over my head and let it fly away on the warm breeze, shivering as the air tickles my skin. Ben pulls off his own shirt and releases it into the wind. I slide off my shorts and release them too. One by one, we release every article of our clothing until we are both completely undressed except for our socks and shoes. Our eyes lock. I feel—

"Ready?" Ben asks.

I shake off my daydream and snap back to the present: Ben and I on horseback—fully clothed—at the top of Mount Hollywood.

"Not really," I say.

But the other horses have already started heading down the mountain. Ben's horse turns to leave. And my horse follows.

* * *

My mouth is dry, and my legs are sore and tired. It has been almost an hour since Ben and I dropped off our horses at the ranch and began our hike up the dusty, shade-free trails that wind their way to the top of Mount Lee, heading toward the Hollywood Sign. Right now, to our right, at the base of the mountain, is a sprawling, grassy cemetery separated from an expansive city by a freeway with cars the size of ants. To our left, Mount Lee rises sharply, shielding Hollywood and the Hollywood Sign from view.

Ben and I have spent most of our hike in silence, aside from the occasional comment about the view. I decide to try to use conversation to distract myself from my aching muscles. "You seemed incredibly comfortable on that horse," I say to him.

"I was," he says, keeping his focus on the path that we climb. "I used to ride competitively. Riding was my life."

"So what happened?"

"It's kind of a long story."

"If you're willing to tell it, I want to hear it."

He glances toward me and then returns his attention to the ground. "Even after that last one?"

"*Especially* after that last one." I feel like every story Ben tells me brings us closer together. I like that feeling, even though it scares me.

Ben pauses along a white wooden fence that separates us from the steep mountainside. He looks into the distance—toward the faint purple mountains that rise up beyond the city—and inhales. "I had this horse: Marge. She was a great horse. The best. On the day of one of my biggest competitions, I noticed that Marge was acting really sensitive. Every little noise bothered her. My father said she must be having a bad day, but she'd never had bad days before. Because of the competition, I had to ride her anyway. At the beginning, she was doing all right. But then she missed a jump. I think that made her upset because on the next one she jumped way too high. When she landed, she lost her footing, and we fell. I hit my head and went unconscious. I woke up in the hospital, but aside from a bad headache, I was fine. When I asked about Marge, my father said she was gone. He'd *sold* her. I was furious. I loved that horse.

"A few months later, I overheard my father telling my mom that it was *her* fault Marge had been spooked that day. Apparently, my mom had forgotten to do something or other for my father and, in front of Marge, they'd had an 'argument'—which is the word that my father used for his one-sided beratings of my mom. I remember that, just before I took Marge out to the arena, when my father came in to wish me good luck, Marge had gotten very upset. I couldn't calm her down. Now I know why: she was afraid of my father. But even once I found out the truth, there was nothing I could do to get her back."

"I'm sorry about your horse," I say. And I add what I should have said earlier, "And I'm sorry your father."

Without a response, Ben turns and starts up the trail again. As we walk, a horrible thought begins to fester in my mind. *I wonder if Ben's 'true stories' are actually true.* He sounded so sincere when he told them, but Ben is a good storyteller. Good storytellers make good liars. Apparently, I'm not good at sensing deception. I trusted Barry. I believed he was my friend. I never thought he could hurt me. But he hurt me in a way no one would ever hurt a friend. Is Ben planning to betray me too? If so, is his motivation the same as Barry's or is he driven by something different?

As we round the next bend, Ben announces, "We made it." He points to a tall chain-link fence along the side of the trail. I go to it and see that the corrugated backsides of the famous Hollywood Sign letters are just below us. The letters look smaller than I thought they would, but it is a thrill to see them this close. Beyond them are mansion-covered hills. Not far away, there's a triangular, blue-green, glistening lake nestled in a valley of extravagant homes. I almost prefer this view to the one at the top of Mount Hollywood. But that view was 360-degrees. I turn around to look for a higher vantage point and notice that the peak of Mount Lee is just a few feet above us.

"Do you think there's a way to get up there?" I ask

Ben.

"There must be."

We continue up the road until it ends at a razor-wire-topped, gated area that houses a collection of tall radio towers. Off to the side is a steep dirt trail. Ben bounds up the path, and I crawl up after him, my sneakers slipping on the loose dirt. The short climb is well worth the effort once we stand at the peak of Mount Lee, captivated by the fence-free view that extends from the Hollywood Sign all the way to the ocean.

Unlike in my daydream, our clothes stay on and Ben's lips stay away from mine. But despite the fact that I barely know him, despite my concerns about his motivations, when I look into Ben's eyes, I feel just as warm and tingly as I did in my imagination, maybe more so.

"I had an amazing day with you, Ben," I say. "Thank you."

"I should be thanking you," he says. "I feel like, tomorrow, I'll actually be able to write something."

"That's great," I say, but my stomach sinks. I'm glad Ben feels ready to write, but I'd thought maybe we would spend another day with each other. I hate to think that today might be the only day we'll ever spend together. Already, I feel the emptiness of a tomorrow without him.

As I stand by Ben's side, admiring the view, I try to will time to slow down. But I feel like it only moves faster.

* * *

At a picnic table under the willow tree in his backyard, Ben and I relive the highlights of our day while devouring take-out Thai food. Once the sun starts to leave the sky and the air begins to chill, we collect our empty containers and head back toward the house, along a meandering stone path lined with white, sweet-smelling flowers.

As we pass the pond-like pool and hot tub, Ben says, "Want to take a dip in the hot tub?"

I imagine sitting with Ben in the bubbly, warm water. The thought makes my skin tingle with excitement, while at the same time it makes my stomach churn. But I hear myself say, "Okay." Strangely, my decision leaves me feeling strong, rather than afraid.

We separate to go put on our swimsuits. I find mine in a plastic bag in the bottom of my backpack. After everything that happened last night, I forgot to rinse it and hang it up. I dig it out and get a whiff of rotten seaweed mixed with mildew. *Ick!* In the bathroom, I try to wash out the stink with soap, but the swimsuit holds onto the horrid odor. I hang it in the shower to air out and return to the backyard still wearing my shorts and t-shirt. Ben is already in the hot tub.

"You changed your mind?" he asks as I approach.

"I forgot to take my swimsuit out of my backpack yesterday. Now it's mildewed." I sit on the edge of the tub and let my bare legs fall into the water.

"You don't have to wear a bathing suit if you don't want to," Ben says nonchalantly.

I look into the bubbles, feeling uneasy. "Aren't *you* wearing a bathing suit?" I can't tell whether he is or not.

"Yes," he says, "but if it makes you feel better, I can take it off." He starts to get up.

"No!" I practically shout.

Ben seems surprised by my emotional response. "Sorry. That was a joke."

Just before he sinks back into the water, I catch a glimpse of a few pink, raised scars on his chest: straight ones, like from surgery, and jagged ones, like from trauma. *Maybe Ben's stories are true.*

Ben notices my gaze. His jaw clenches, and he looks down at the water.

"I have scars too," I say. "You just can't see them."

He doesn't look up. "I know."

But he doesn't know the source of my scars. Ben has told me his horrible, dark secrets. I want to let him know mine. I make another decision. The bravest one I've made so far. "May I tell you a story?"

He looks at me, his forehead creased. "Okay."

"It's a true story," I say.

He nods.

I focus my eyes on the bubbles in the water. I'm not sure where to start my story. And so I start at the end, "There was this guy named Barry." Without lifting my gaze from the water, I tell Ben about the night Barry hurt me. How Barry held me down with his heavy body and pressed a pillow over my face until I couldn't breathe. How, when Barry forced himself on me, it felt like he was stabbing my insides, all the way down to my soul. How, ever since then, some touches are exquisitely painful. "Even if someone brushes against me by accident, it can feel like I'm being cut with a thousand knives. That's why I don't want you to touch me." I pause for a moment, feeling the loss of those moments. The loss of comforting touches between two people. "I'm so broken, Ben."

He inhales. "Life changes us, but it can only break us if we let it."

I finally look at him. His face shows no judgment. And no pity. Just certainty.

I make another decision, one that scares me to death. "Close your eyes," I say.

Ben looks at me. "Why?"

"Do you trust me?" I ask.

"Yes, I do." He closes his eyes tightly.

I pull my shirt up over my head and drape it on a chair. I unzip my shorts and put them on the seat. I consider stopping here, but I feel like I must go further. I can't do this partway. I remove my bra and drop it on top of my shorts. I slip off my panties and toss them there too. Then I step into the churning water. It feels hot. Too hot. But I go deeper. The scalding water meets my thighs. It hurts, but I sink lower, allowing the water to embrace my abdomen and then my chest. But instead of the burning pain overwhelming my senses, the water starts to feel soothing.

"You can open your eyes now," I say to Ben.

He opens his eyes, and his gaze goes to the chair. To my clothes. And then to me. But only to my face. Once his eyes are focused on me, they don't stray at all. I wonder if he can see how vulnerable I feel. We sit in silence, just looking into each other's eyes.

Finally, Ben pulls himself out of the hot tub and sits on the edge. He's wearing plain navy-blue swim trunks. His chest is rippled with perfect muscles, like a model's, but his skin is marked all over with scars. So many of them. Violating his beautiful body. The scars of his childhood. They hurt me as if they are my own. I feel like there's something I need to do. Not just for me, but for both of us.

"May I hug you?" I ask Ben.

His shoulders tense. "Now?" he asks.

"Is that okay?"

He inhales uncomfortably. "I don't think it's a good idea, Erin."

"Please." I look into his eyes, desperate. "I *need* to do this."

Ben holds my gaze for a long time, then he exhales and says, "Do whatever you need to do."

Maybe I'm not ready for this or maybe I am. I don't care. I swim across the hot tub and climb up onto the seat. I stand in front of Ben, afraid to touch him, afraid of how it will feel. My heart races. My breaths quicken. My body trembles. All I can think about is fear. *I HATE that fear.*

I need to do this now, even if it kills me.

I close my eyes and wrap my arms around Ben as tightly as I can. He wraps his arms around me just as tightly. I feel our hearts pounding. I feel our chests rise and fall. I feel the heat radiating from his skin to mine. But I don't feel *any* pain.

I stay there in Ben's arms. Until I stop trembling.

Chapter Nine

I awaken to the muffled sound of someone typing fast on a keyboard. I inhale a pleasant lungful of peach potpourri and hop out of the heavenly princess bed. When I open the guest room door, I accidentally kick the squeaky cat toy—the one I used as an intruder detector on my first night in Ben's house—all the way into the living room. I didn't wedge it under my door before I went to bed last night. Probably that's because, when Ben held my naked body in his arms at the hot tub, all he did was hug me. Nothing more. He didn't try to kiss me. His hands never strayed from my back.

I walk quietly to Ben's doorway, and I watch him type. He looks the way he did when I first saw him in the coffee shop, only now he wears blue checked boxers, brown socks, and a faded gray t-shirt. After a few minutes, he finally looks up at me.

"Are you *writing*?" I ask.

"Yes," he says.

I try to read his expression, but I can't. "For real?"

"Yes." He smiles, the relief washing over his face.

I run to him. "Can I see?"

Ben takes me by the waist and spins me away from the screen. "Not yet."

I stare at him and he stares at me. I don't breathe. Ben's hands remain on my hips as if they belong there. I am suddenly aware that my nightshirt has shifted down to reveal a hint of my chest. But instead of feeling vulnerable, I feel … electrified.

"Well then, I'm going to go have breakfast," I say.

He nods and takes his hands from my waist. "I'm almost done with this scene. I'll be there in a few minutes."

As I leave the room, I hear Ben clicking away again. It's comforting.

I find Bolt lying on the living room floor, vigorously attempting to disembowel the cat toy mouse with his back claws. As soon as I enter the room, he discards the toy and runs to me, purring loudly. I pet him for a minute, and then he walks off to the kitchen where he crunches on some cat kibble. I grab the almond butter and granola and half-watch the news. There was a big car accident on the 101 Freeway. Nobody died, but traffic is pretty backed up.

I'm pouring granola over a mound of almond butter when Ben enters the kitchen, fills a glass of water, and sits down at the table. "So what are your plans for today?" he asks.

"I thought I'd go to Griffith Park. I want to take a ride on the Live Steamers model train and then check out the Los Angeles Zoo."

"How are you going to get there?"

"The bus," I say, taking a bite of granola.

"If you can drive a stick-shift, you can borrow the car." Ben points to a nearby door. "The keys are on the hook over there."

I force the granola down my throat with a mouthful of water. "You're offering to let me borrow *your car*?" I ask, incredulous.

He shrugs. "It's my father's car."

Okay, but still ... "What if I drive off and never come back?"

He shakes his head. "You won't."

I cock my head, skeptical. "How do you know that?"

"I know *you*."

Is it possible that Ben really does trust me? Maybe, even without fully knowing me, something deep inside him makes him certain that I would never willingly harm him. The way I trust him.

"Besides," he adds, "if you did steal that car, no one would miss it anyway." He grabs a breakfast bar from the cabinet and heads back down the hallway. And then I hear him shut his bedroom door.

* * *

After I finish my breakfast, I get dressed in a pair of brown shorts and a plain gray t-shirt, an outfit that makes me feel as if I can be nearly invisible if I want to be. Then I take the keychain that hangs from a hook in the kitchen and go to Ben's bedroom to let him know I'm leaving. His door is open now, but I don't see him inside the room. I knock on the doorjamb. "Ben?"

"One second," Ben calls out from a room attached to his. Almost exactly one second later, he comes around the corner, easing a plain white t-shirt over his glistening, freshly-washed hair.

"I just wanted to wish you a good day writing," I say, averting my eyes from his scarred chest. It still hurts me to look at his scars, even though, whether I see them or not, I will always know they're there.

"Would you mind if I join you today?" Ben asks.

I smile knowingly. "You had second thoughts about me driving off with the car, didn't you?"

"No. I've been writing since three in the morning. I think I'm done for now," he says. "So what do you think? Do you want company?"

My heart pounds with excitement. "Absolutely."

Ben stuffs his wallet into his pocket and follows me to the garage. When I open the door, I do a double take. Morning sunlight sparkles off a sleek, black, spotless sports car. I don't know much about cars, but this one looks extremely expensive. I try to pass the keychain to Ben, but he pushes it away.

"Aren't you going to drive?" I ask.

"I can't," Ben says. "Not legally anyway. My father never let me get a driver's license."

But his father is gone now. I wonder why Ben didn't get a license after he left. Instead of asking, I open the leather pouch attached to the keychain and take out a car door remote with a crystal tip. I unlock the doors and slide into the driver's seat as Ben slips into the passenger's seat. The seat cradles my body perfectly.

There's no key on the keychain and so I search the dash for some sort of ignition button. Finding none, I ask Ben, "How do I start the car?"

Ben points to the door remote. "That's the key."

"What do I *do* with it?"

"Put it there." Ben gestures to an unlikely location on the front dash.

I push the crystal "key" into the dash and the engine revs to life. I grin.

"That's the button for the roof," Ben says, pointing to another button.

"The roof ...?" I start to say as I press the button Ben indicated. Soundlessly, the car's roof folds back and hides itself in the trunk. Suddenly, I have a new appreciation for cars. "This car is awesome!" I say. And then I remember whose car this is. "Sorry, I—"

"It's okay," Ben says. "The car *is* awesome."

"Why didn't your father take it with him?"

"He drove off in his other one and we never heard from him again." From Ben's tone, I can sense the hurt he feels. As horrible as his father was to him and his mom, I'm sure part of Ben loves him. "Anyway, my mom won't drive this thing, and I can't, so today, I'm going to drive it vicariously through you. Okay?"

I smile. "Okay."

I put my hand on the shifter. Ben puts his hand on top of mine. Tingles of electricity run up my arm and into my chest. I take a deep breath and shift the car into first gear.

* * *

Ben's father's car glides effortlessly over the road, almost as if it's flying. I never really enjoyed driving before, but driving *this* car is fun. We leave Ben's neighborhood behind and travel the tree-lined roads of Griffith Park. It isn't long before we arrive at the Live Steamers model train place. From the road, I spot a diminutive bridge and doll-sized buildings on the other side of some chain-link fencing.

I pull into the parking lot across the street and park in a far corner—that's what my father always did with his cars to keep them from getting dinged by other people's car doors. And none of my father's cars were nearly as impressive as this one.

The train place hasn't opened yet, and so Ben and I join the queue of about ten people outside the gate. A woman handing juice boxes to twin toddlers in a double stroller turns toward us as we arrive. She looks down, as if looking for a child. Finding none, she gives me a tight-lipped acknowledgement and looks away. We are the only people here without at least one little kid, but the reviews online said that these trains were great, even for adults. I hope they're right.

A squat, grandfatherly man wearing a train conductor's hat hobbles over and opens the gate. The small crowd moves inside quickly, parents holding the hands of their straining children. We buy our tickets and then walk through a series of switchbacks to a small train. Little kids and their adults straddle the padded cars. I take a seat toward the back of the train. Ben slides in behind me.

A little girl races down the length of the train, followed by her hurrying mother, and climbs onto the train just in front of me.

"I'm sorry," her mom says to me, squishing in behind her daughter.

"No problem," I assure her.

I have to scoot back so far that I am practically sitting in Ben's lap. With no room left for his hands, Ben lightly rests them on my thighs. "Is that okay?" he whispers.

"Yeah, that's okay." After last night's experience in the hot tub, having Ben's hands on my thighs doesn't upset me. I actually like it a little.

The train pulls away from the station and picks up speed, moving faster than I'd thought it would. We travel over a bridge and past a tiny western town. As we go through an echoey tunnel, I decide to experiment with my new comfort zone with Ben. I place my hands on top of his. Tingling radiates up my arms. He spreads his fingers and I press my fingers between them. It feels almost more intimate than our nearly-naked hug last night, although I'm not sure how that could be. Maybe it's because, as our fingers lace together, they bring with them everything we've experienced up until now, including that hug. We spend the rest of the ride like this.

When we arrive back at the station, two small boys on the train car in front of us shout, "Again! Again!" I want to shout it too, but of course, I don't.

"To the zoo?" Ben asks as we get up.

"To the zoo," I say, feeling cold where our bodies are no longer touching.

And then I remember that I get to drive that awesome car again. That cheers me up a little. But not enough.

* * *

Our fellow zoogoers are captivated by whatever is on the other side of the chest-high wall ahead of us. A couple moves away, and Ben and I slip into their place. Below the wall is a landscaped area with rocks, trees, logs, a stream, and a beautiful adult tiger striding along a dirt path. Without warning, a tiger cub leaps out from behind a log and pounces on her. The adult tiger brushes off the attack and continues on her way. Another cub launches a second attack that hardly seems to register with the adult, who keeps going toward the back of the enclosure. The first cub pounces on the second one. The second cub rolls onto his back, swatting at the first cub with his oversized paws. Then they switch roles and the pouncer becomes the pouncee.

I pull out my camera and zoom in to capture the little tigers' faces. After I get a few good shots, I put the camera away, and lean against the wall, watching the cubs play. Ben moves behind me, making room for a man holding a little girl in his arms.

"Kitties!" the girl exclaims as she catches her first glimpse of the tigers.

"No, they're not *kitties*. Those are *tigers*," the man corrects her with a cold tone that makes my body stiffen.

The little girl, who can't be more than three years old, probably can't tell the difference. "Kitties!" the girl says once more.

The man shakes his head. "They're *tigers*. And you're a ditz just like your mother."

He puts the girl on the ground. The child climbs onto a step, but without her father's help, she can't see over the wall. "Kitties! Kitties!" she cries, frantically holding her arms out to her father, begging him to pick her up again so she can see the cubs.

Ben's right hand forms into a tight fist as he glares at the father ignoring his child's cries. Sensing trouble, I take Ben's other hand and lead him away.

"Were you going to punch him?" I ask as soon as we're far enough away that the man can't hear us.

"No," Ben says, as if he's disappointed in himself.

"He reminds you of your father?" I ask.

"Yeah."

"He reminds me of my father too," I say, instantly regretting that I said it.

"That's the first time you've said anything about your family."

"I don't like talking about my family."

"Me neither."

But Ben has already shared so much about his family. And so I take a breath and tell him, "Every morning, even on Saturdays and Sundays, my father gets up, goes to work, comes home, plays games on his computer for a few hours, and then goes to bed. He never wanted to have much to do with me. I tried to make him proud. I didn't get into trouble. I did well in school, but when I gave him my report cards to sign, he didn't even read them. I taught myself chess because it was my father's favorite game, but he never wanted to play with me.

"On the night of my prom, I called my father to see if

he would pick me up from Barry's apartment. Before I could even tell him why I was calling, he said that I woke him up, and it was too late to be calling him, unless it was a life-threatening emergency. He asked me if I had a life-threatening emergency. I said, 'No.' Then I told Barry that I would spend the night with him." Horrible memories come rushing up. I swallow them down. "Of course I don't blame my father for what happened with Barry. What happened that night was my fault."

"No," Ben says. "What happened that night was *Barry's* fault."

Ben and I continue down a path to a giant makeshift jungle gym surrounded by netting, where reddish-brown orangutans use their gangly arms to deftly scale a network of ropes. On the ground, a tiny orangutan is cradled in the arms of an adult—probably his mother.

The baby reaches toward a nearby rope. His fingertips barely touch it. The mother orangutan gives him what looks like a hug and then loosens her embrace enough that, when the baby reaches again, his tiny fingers wrap around the rope. He pulls himself toward it, almost wriggling out of his mother's arms, but then seems to reconsider. He lets go of the rope and grabs hold of his mother.

"Does your father know you're here alone in L.A.?" Ben asks.

"I told him I was going on a trip. He didn't ask for details."

"What about your mom?"

"I can't tell her anything anymore …"

"Why not?"

I stare at the orangutan cuddling her baby, the way my mother used to cuddle me. "Because I have no idea where my mother is."

* * *

A hoofed animal balances on her impossibly-delicate hind legs and nibbles at some leaves on a tree. According to a sign, she's a gerenuk.

Another gerenuk stands nearby, chewing. When she swallows, a small bulge appears at the top of her long, skinny neck and travels down, disappearing into her body. A moment later, the bulge reappears at the bottom of her neck and travels back up. She starts chewing again.

"You can *see* them regurgitate!" I exclaim.

Ben laughs.

My cheeks flush. "Sorry, I guess that's kind of gross."

"I think it's cool." Ben smiles enough that his dimple shows. "Speaking of regurgitation, are you hungry?"

"Getting there." I look at my watch. *It's almost four-thirty.* I wonder where the day went.

"We could go to dinner at CityWalk!" Ben suggests.

CityWalk is an open-air shopping mall that looks as if it was ripped out of a cartoon world and dropped into reality. During our trip to L.A., Star and I spent an evening at CityWalk after a day at Universal Studios Hollywood theme park. We ate at Saddle Ranch Chop House. After dinner, Star rode the mechanical bull in the center of their dining room for a full minute while everyone cheered her on. Then we wandered in and out of the sweet shops and souvenir stores and shared a deliciously-gooey cinnamon bun for dessert. It was a perfect day.

I had been planning to go to CityWalk on this trip too, but after my recent experiences at the observatory and the beach, I'd rather go someplace else, *anyplace else* than a place I visited with Star.

But Ben seems so enthused about CityWalk that I say, "Okay."

* * *

We ask the car's GPS to guide us from the zoo to CityWalk. Once we've entered our destination, it speaks: "Depart," the GPS says, in the menacing voice of Darth Vader. "Your destiny lies with me."

"What's with the Darth Vader GPS?" I ask Ben.

"When I was seven, I put him on there as a joke. My father never took him off."

Darth Vader takes a noisy breath. "Turn to the left."

I smile. "I like it."

Darth directs me onto the freeway. My hands sweat as I shift into fourth gear and merge with the fast-moving traffic. It has been a while since I drove this fast. I got my driver's license two years ago, but I've never really used it. If it hadn't been for Star's dad, I probably wouldn't have bothered getting my license at all, and I certainly wouldn't have learned to drive a stick-shift. When Star's dad was teaching her to drive, Star invited me to come along and he taught me too. He insisted that we learn to drive a stick before he'd let us "be lazy" with an automatic. Although I had no real interest in driving, I looked forward to those lessons with Star and her dad. Star's dad was enthusiastic and supportive. He was everything my father wasn't.

"Take the exit right. Do not fail me this time," the GPS says, channeling Darth. "Turn to the right and then proceed as indicated. Don't make me destroy you."

I turn onto Lankershim Boulevard and head south, making the first light but missing the next one. I roll to a stop at an intersection with a large church on the corner: Saint Charles Borromeo Church. People mill about on the sidewalk in front of it. News reporters talk to their cameras. And then I remember: *Alexis's funeral is today.*

"That must be the funeral for the girl who drowned at the beach," I say to Ben.

He looks out the window. "Yeah, it must be."

Did Ben know that we'd pass this church on our way to CityWalk? Is he trying to trick me into going to the funeral? I feel my pulse rise. "Is this why you wanted to go to CityWalk?"

He looks into my eyes. "No."

"So you're saying it's just a coincidence that we ended up here?" I ask.

"Or fate," he says.

I shake my head. "I don't believe in fate."

Ben exhales. "Well, I do," he says softly.

The traffic light turns green. Behind me, someone taps their car horn. I drive forward, but instead of continuing straight down the road to CityWalk, I turn into the church parking lot.

"Turn around when possible," Darth Vader growls. "I find your lack of faith disturbing."

I silence the protesting GPS and park the car in the first empty space that I see, and then I sit, staring at the steering wheel. "I want to go to the funeral," I finally say.

Ben turns toward me. "Really?"

"Yes."

"I thought you hate funerals."

I swallow. "I do."

Chapter Ten

The church is packed with slack-faced people mourning a girl I never knew. Still, maybe I should be here. For Alexis. Although Alexis and I never met in life, I was the first person she met in death.

There are no unoccupied seats inside the church, and so Ben and I find a spot to stand against a side wall. A dark-haired woman at the lectern fights back tears as she talks about how Alexis volunteered at a hospital every weekend, leading art projects to cheer up the sick patients. The closed coffin behind the woman is covered in tiny pink and white flowers. Beside it, there is a framed photo of a bright, vibrant girl, but when I look at the coffin, I see Alexis's bloated, purple body.

My gaze jumps to someone standing in the shadow of the wooden altar that makes up the entire front wall of the church. A girl. She wasn't there a moment ago. It's as if she magically appeared. Her long brown hair is neatly pulled back, and she's wearing a black jacket and skirt. I recognize her instantly: *Alexis*.

Of course Alexis isn't really there. I'm imagining her. Just like I sometimes imagine Star.

The first time I imagined Star was on the day of her funeral. I didn't go to Star's funeral because I always thought that funerals are for the living rather than the dead. And I felt like the *living* people who would be at Star's funeral—especially Star's mom and dad—didn't want me there.

While everyone was at the church, I trudged along the deserted sidewalks of our neighborhood. When I arrived at Star's house, I stopped and stared at the lawn that her father used to mow every Saturday, whether it needed mowing or not. Now it was overgrown. It had been untouched since Star died. I wiped away tears, and when I looked back, I saw Star sitting cross-legged in the scraggly grass, as if she were waiting for me. My heart nearly stopped.

Star looked just like she did in life, as if she was really there, but she looked at me in a way she never had before. Her eyes pierced right through me, unblinking, as if she was furious with me. Did she blame me for her death, the way everyone else seemed to, the way I blamed myself? I stared at her image, wishing I could will her back to life. And then, involuntarily, I blinked. When my eyes reopened, Star was gone. I whispered, "I'm sorry," and then turned and walked back home.

Alexis is looking at me the same way Star did that day.

Her gaze penetrates my brain, making my head throb with each beat of my accelerating heart. My breaths come fast. My palms sweat. My legs grow so weak that they can no longer support my weight. I look away from Alexis, trying to keep her eyes from boring into me, but I still feel them. I lean against the wall and try to focus on the speaker's words, but it's all I can do keep myself upright.

Calm down, Erin. You need to calm down. I force myself to inhale deeply and count in my head, *One Mississippi, Two Mississippi, Three ... this isn't working. One Mississippi, Two Mississippi ... I can't do this. One Mississippi, Two ... I CAN'T BREATHE!* My eyes won't focus. My brain feels like it's drowning. *I have to get out of here.*

"I need ... some air," I say to Ben.

"I'll come with you," he says.

"Please stay," I say without looking at him.

I make my way toward the exit, whispering hurried apologies to the people in my path. Finally, I heave open the heavy door and rush down a corridor, keeping one hand on the wall, so I don't collapse. I can't go outside like this, with all the camera and news people out there. I need to go somewhere where I can be alone. I find the ladies' room and lock myself inside a stall, then sitting on the toilet, I press my fingers hard against my temples, trying to stop the unrelenting pounding in my head.

* * *

It feels like I've been in the restroom stall for hours, but my watch indicates that only ten minutes have passed. Even though my heart is beating calmly and I'm breathing normally, I don't feel ready to go back to the funeral. But I must. Ben is surely worried about me.

I open the stall, but before I can exit, what I see chokes all of the air from my lungs. Standing at a sink, staring at my reflection in the mirror, tears dripping down her face, is *Alexis*.

But it can't be. Alexis is gone.

"Alexis?" I say anyway.

The girl looks as pained as if I just punched her in the heart. "Diana," she says.

I don't understand. "Diana?"

"I'm Alexis's sister," she says. "We're ... twins."

And now it makes sense. Air returns to my lungs. "I'm so very sorry for your loss." It's what people said to me when they found out I'd lost Star. These words don't provide much comfort, but as much as I desperately try, I can't think of anything to say that would provide any real solace. I wash my hands and then dry them with a paper towel.

"Did you know her?" Diana asks me, looking at her feet.

"I was swimming in the ocean on the day she was found."

Her big eyes lock on mine. "Did you see the girl who found her?"

"*I* was the girl who found her," I admit.

Her gaze searches my face for far too long before she speaks again. "Do you think she was scared when she died?" she asks, her voice unsteady.

I remember Alexis's bloated face, her mouth stretched open in a silent scream. I think Alexis *was* scared. How could she not have been? But I can't say that to her sister. I want to spare her. "I don't know," I say.

"Alexis saved my life. I should have been the one who died." Her face contorts and her body begins to shake with soundless sobs.

I can't comfort this girl. I don't know how. I wish I could say something to bring her peace, but when someone you love dies before they truly had a chance to live, there is no peace. Or if there is, I haven't found it.

After Star died, I wondered whether it would have been better if I'd died instead of her. Star was so much smarter than me. She was better at school and sports. She had more friends than me. Her life had so much more potential than mine. I read that it's called "survivor's guilt," and it's normal, but it feels so gut-wrenchingly terrible that it makes going on living hard to bear. "After my best friend, Star, passed away, I wished I was the one who died," I say. I don't tell her that I still feel that way.

I place my hand against the door, about to leave. But

then I have an idea of how I might comfort this girl. If only I can make myself do it. If only I am strong enough. I take a deep breath and turn around.

"Is it okay if I hug you?" I ask her.

"Yes," she says. "That would be okay."

I swallow my fear and walk to Diana. I take another deep breath, drawing up all of my strength, and I put my arms around her, the way Ben did to me last night. And I let her cry.

Maybe it is possible for people to find peace after their lives have been shattered. Maybe it's possible for people to heal from horrific trauma. I hope this girl is able to heal. Maybe it's possible for me to heal as well.

After a few minutes, Diana whispers, "Thank you for finding Alexis."

I take hold of both her hands—the way Star and I used to do when we told each other something really important—and I look into Diana's eyes. "Alexis was lucky to have someone in her life who cared about her so much."

She gives a small nod. "Star was lucky too."

I give her a nod in response. There is nothing more to say. I turn and walk to the bathroom door, push it open, and step into the corridor. But it isn't the corridor I left minutes ago. It is now filled with a suffocating sea of people.

They pour from the church doors and surge toward me. I feel as if I'm submerged in a tumultuous ocean, fighting for air and finding none. Drowning. *If I keep walking, I won't drown.* I try to force myself to take a step, but my legs won't carry me forward. It's as if my joints have frozen solid. Fear has rendered me immobile.

Bodies hit me like fiery embers. I want to scream, but when I open my mouth, no sound comes. Burning pain singes my violated skin and stabs deep into my insides. Overwhelming me. Incinerating me. I close my eyes and try frantically to make my body numb. Unfeeling. Dead.

And then Ben's hand lands on my shoulder. Somehow I feel it through the pain. I surrender to him. He urges me forward, and I take a step. And then another one. And another one. Each step I take makes me feel stronger. More alive. Someone brushes against me. It burns, but it's tolerable. I keep going. Because of Ben. Because someone cares.

A rush of air blasts against my skin. Warm light spreads across my face. I open my eyes and find myself on the sidewalk outside the church. I suck in a breath, as if I just surfaced from underwater. Ben's hand squeezes my shoulder. I turn toward him. But he isn't there.

He never was.

Diana is standing next to me, her hand still on my shoulder. She doesn't speak, but her eyes ask many questions and my eyes provide at least some of the answers. "Thank you" are the only words I say aloud. Diana offers a very small smile and then turns and walks back into the church.

An instant later, Ben rushes out of the building, his face tense. The tension doesn't fade when he spots me. "I've been looking everywhere for you," he says, running up to me. "What happened?" He doesn't seem angry, just concerned.

I look away from him. "Let's just … go to dinner."

We walk to the car in silence. Once we are on our way toward CityWalk, I tell Ben everything that happened to me in the church. Absolutely everything.

* * *

The last time I was at CityWalk, the large gleaming silver globe in the misty fountain at the entrance looked welcoming. Now it looks foreboding. Even the glamorous red carpet that leads to the towering arched entrance of Universal Studios theme park doesn't appeal to me.

"What are you in the mood for?" Ben asks me.

"I want to ride the mechanical bull at Saddle Ranch Chop House," I say.

His forehead wrinkles with bewilderment. "I didn't think you were the mechanical-bull-riding type."

"I'm not."

"Why do you want to do it then?" he asks.

I haven't told Ben much about Star yet. I think it's time. "A little over a year ago, I took a trip to Los Angeles with my best friend, Star. She's the one who died. The one whose funeral I didn't go to …" I draw up some strength and I continue, "Riding that bull was something Star wanted me to do. When we were here. But I didn't. So now I'm going to do it. For her."

"Okay," Ben says softly.

A perky man in jeans and a Saddle Ranch t-shirt greets us at the restaurant entrance. "Here for dinner?"

"Yes," I say. "But I want to ride the bull first." *Before I change my mind.*

He smiles broadly. "Awesome. Head on back."

I know exactly where to go. Just as the bull comes into view, I see a woman wearing a spaghetti-strap top and a short skirt fall off it. Men cheer and whistle. I have second and third thoughts about doing this, but I push them aside and approach the ring as the previous rider rejoins her exuberant girlfriends at their table.

"Wanna ride?" the man running the bull asks me.

"Yeah," I say.

He hands me a waiver form on a clipboard. I don't bother reading it. It doesn't matter what it says. I'm going to sign it anyway. I hand the signed paper back to him, and the man leads me onto the bouncy mats surrounding the bull. I try to ignore the people leaning on the tables at the edge of the ring. Talking. Drinking. Laughing. *Watching me.*

"Climb on up," the bull operator says.

I stare at the thick, padded mound that loosely resembles a bull. Threatening-looking horns protrude from its head. I remember watching Star ride the bull. The bull shook and bucked and threw her in all different directions for a full minute, but she never fell off. She wouldn't let go.

"That was so fun," Star had said to me afterward, breathless and bursting with adrenaline. "You've gotta try it!"

"I just ate. I don't want to vomit." That was just an excuse and Star knew it.

"If you don't want to do it, just say so."

"I *do* want to do it. It seems fun. But I don't want to look ridiculous." That was the truth.

Star took both of my hands in hers. "Erin, if you want to do something, don't let anyone or anything stop you."

I shook my head. "Maybe next time."

"What if there isn't a next time?"

"I'm sure there will be," I said.

But I was wrong. There will never be a next time. Not for Star and me.

I take a breath and mount the bull.

"Keep one hand in the air," the bull operator says. "Have a good time!"

Men clap and hoot. I want to close my eyes and make them all go away, but instead I search among the people, looking for Ben. I find him standing quietly, apart from the boisterous crowd. I hold his gaze ... and then the bull whips around in a circle, instantly disorienting me.

I grip onto the bull with my right hand and my legs.

The bull bucks forward and back. I make my ears go deaf and concentrate on riding him. He shakes. He dips. He spins. Violently. So violently. I feel myself slipping. I feel dizzy. I could let myself fall. If I fall, it's over. But that's the easy way out. Star wouldn't have approved. In the entire time I knew her, she only took the easy way out once. Just once.

I hold onto the bull as if death awaits me on the padded mats below it. *I won't let go. I will never let go.*

And then the bull slows to a stop. Cheers break through the silence in my head.

The bull operator runs up to me and offers his hand. "Great job!" he says.

"Thanks," I mumble. My arms and legs trembling, I climb off the bull without his help.

Ben meets me at the ring exit. "That was amazing, Erin!" he says, gushing with enthusiasm. "You did the entire minute. And they didn't go easy on you. Let's get a table and celebrate."

"Can we just go?" I ask.

Ben looks into my eyes. "All right."

By the time we get into the car, I'm crying—despite my attempts not to. I close the door and drop my face into my hands. "I'm sorry, Ben," I say. "You wanted to eat there and—"

"I don't care about eating," he says. "I can go all night without eating."

My tears stop at Ben's selflessness.

"So what happened in there?" he continues.

"All those people staring at me. It was terrifying." I inhale, and then ... I smile. "But I did it. I rode the bull."

"Then why were you crying?"

"I miss Star so much. She made me want to *really* experience life. To squeeze out every drop of adventure ... You make me feel that way too." I stare into his eyes for a moment before I go on, "I feel like I'm connecting with you in a way I've never connected with anyone else. Not even Star. I hardly know you, but I feel like I've known you my entire life."

"I feel the same way." Ben strokes my cheek, wiping away the tears.

I close my eyes and allow myself to experience the warmth of his fingers on my face. Heat builds inside me. Along with intense, overwhelming fear. I *want* Ben. I want him in a way I've never wanted anyone else. I want his lips to press against mine. I want to feel his hands on my body. I want to feel him deep inside me. And it's more than a *want*. It's a *need*. Like the need for air. A need that surpasses all others.

But I am so scared.

"I'm starving," I blurt out. I *am* starving. But no food will satisfy me.

"I know a great Italian place," Ben suggests.

"Okay."

* * *

It is as if we're dining in old-world Italy. The three-dimensional murals covering the inner walls of Miceli's restaurant immerse us in the atmosphere of a charming Italian neighborhood, complete with a real-life couple dining on a protruding balcony and an artist's rendering of a cat exploring the rooftops. We sit at a booth next to the pianist, whose fingers dance over black and white keys, playing vaguely-familiar music. *Star would have loved it here.* I wish we'd known about this restaurant during our visit.

"You don't like this place?" Ben asks, trying to read my expression.

I look into his eyes. "I absolutely *love* it."

A man deposits a basket on our table. I lift the cloth napkin covering it and find warm rolls inside. I take one. With my first bite through the soft crust and into the doughy center, my appetite surges with a vengeance. *I could eat a hundred of these rolls.*

The waiter who took our order a few moments ago emerges from the kitchen. He whispers something to the pianist and then picks up a microphone. I wonder if he is going to make some sort of announcement, but then the pianist starts a new song and the waiter begins *to sing.* Another waiter grabs a second microphone and joins him in a song about the obstacles that fairytale princes face when pursuing love.

I am delighted until the men saunter over to our booth and start singing directly to me. My cheeks burn with embarrassment, but Ben smiles at me encouragingly. I try to pretend that I'm enjoying myself ... until I finally am.

The waiters continue on around the restaurant, singing to other people: a woman who nods her head in time to the music, a shy little boy who hides behind his menu, a man who joins the waiters in singing a few lines.

The final note of the song, which the waiters hold much longer than they should be able to, is met with enthusiastic applause and, soon after, the delivery of our dinners. We both ordered the eggplant cacciatore, which Ben said is excellent here. And it is.

"This just might be my favorite restaurant," I say.

Ben smiles. "Why?"

It takes me a minute before I can figure out an explanation. "I feel like we've traveled somewhere far away."

Ben laughs. "To a land where waiters sing?"

"To a place where I feel happy."

I twist my chopped eggplant and sliced peppers together into another saucy cluster of deliciousness on my fork, as two waitresses step up to the piano for a duet.

The song is about how people need someone in their life who helps them grow, and who they help in return. In my life, everyone I've let deep into my heart has ultimately hurt me: my mother, my father, Barry, and even Star. I can't think of anyone who has changed my life for the better. Maybe Ben could be that person. I need him to be. He's my last chance.

And given the sadness that I see in his eyes sometimes, I might be his.

* * *

Our dinner at Miceli's improves my mood so much that even the famous Los Angeles traffic that we encounter a few minutes after heading on our way doesn't get me down.

I'm feeling bold, so I ask Ben, "Will you be joining me tomorrow?"

He smiles. "What will we be doing?"

I'd had my whole itinerary planned. I was going to take the Metro to Union Station. After I strolled around the historic train station, I was planning to visit the charming Mexican shops of Olivera Street. Around lunchtime, I'd have dim sum in Chinatown and, after spending the afternoon wandering about in downtown L.A., I'd stop for a dinner of ramen noodles in Little Tokyo. This was how Star and I spent our final day in Los Angeles. But now I feel like I should leave these experiences as memories. I want tomorrow to be not for me, or for Star, but for Ben.

"If you had only one more day to spend here in L.A., how would you spend it?" I ask him.

He thinks for a moment. "I'd go for a hike in Malibu

Creek State Park. That's where they filmed the TV show *M*A*S*H* and the original *Planet of the Apes* movie."

"That sounds cool," I say.

But Ben isn't finished. "Then I'd go to Point Dume Beach in Malibu. There are tide pools there with anemones and gigantic starfish."

"Wow," I say.

He goes on, "I'd finish the night at Griffith Observatory where I'd go to a planetarium show, and then take a look through the Zeiss telescope on the roof."

"That's what I want to do tomorrow," I say, because, suddenly, I can't imagine wanting to spend my last day in Los Angeles any other way.

We round a bend and the traffic thickens. "Looks like there's a show at the Bowl tonight," Ben says.

"A show at the what?"

"The Hollywood Bowl," he says. "It's an enormous stadium where they have concerts. I wonder who's performing."

And then I see the sign. "John Williams, Maestro of the Movies, Tonight 8 PM," I read.

"John Williams wrote the music for *Star Wars*!" Ben says, beaming with excitement.

"And *Harry Potter*!" I add. "We should go to the concert!"

"It's probably sold out."

"I'm willing to take my chances." That doesn't sound

like something I would say, but those words spring from my lips.

"Great!" Ben says.

* * *

According to the apologetic woman at the ticket counter, there are about ten thousand seats in the Hollywood Bowl and tonight every one of them was spoken for ... until she refreshed her computer screen one last time, and two tickets became available. It must have been fate, if you believe in that kind of thing, which I am starting to.

Our seats are in the uppermost tier of the enormous arena, the furthest seats from the stage. Some people might call them "the nosebleed seats," but I think they're great. From here we can see that the Hollywood Bowl is nestled at the base of a bunch of mountains. On one of the distant mountains is the Hollywood Sign. Someone standing right now on the top of Mount Lee, above the Hollywood Sign letters, would be able to see us here—if they had really powerful binoculars.

The sky is darkening by the time John Williams takes the stage. He's so far away that he appears to be just a few millimeters tall. We stand and place our hands over our hearts as he conducts the miniature orchestra playing "The Star Spangled Banner."

When we take our seats again, the night air feels cold on my bare arms and legs. Ben moves closer to me as the orchestra begins to play music from *Harry Potter*. As the music stimulates my imagination, I see us all sitting in a gigantic Great Hall, with an enchanted starry sky for a ceiling. I wish I had magic powers like Harry, Ron, and Hermione. Life would be so much easier with magic powers. Then again, no matter how powerful you are, there's always an evil Voldemort ready to try to destroy you.

Cheer-filled applause pulls me out of my thoughts. When the roar finally dies down, the orchestra begins to play again. With the first few notes, an excited murmur washes over the crowd. Beams of light illuminate the darkness as hundreds of people, including the quiet guy in glasses next to me, activate toy lightsabers and wave them above their heads in time to the music. I can't help but grin at the spectacle.

I glance over to see Ben's reaction and find him already looking at me. Everything around him is a blur, with only Ben in focus. I am drawn to him, as if by some inescapable force. Instead of my body tensing, it completely relaxes. We move closer and closer together. I close my eyes and our lips touch. Lightly. So lightly. I feel the heat of Ben's tremulous breaths. His lips explore mine, hungry, yet gentle. We kiss what feels like a thousand times, but I wish I could kiss him a million more.

Sudden applause thunders around us, and we lean back into our seats, dazed. And then I notice the guy next to me, holding his still-illuminated lightsaber, his mouth hanging open, eyes wide with shock.

"Sorry," I say to the guy, my cheeks hot.

"Yeah. Sorry, man," Ben says.

The guy looks away nervously. "That's okay," he says, switching off and retracting his saber.

Ben and I look at each other. My cheeks still burn with self-consciousness, but despite that, I smile.

* * *

After the John Williams concert, complete with two encores, we cascade out of the Hollywood Bowl, riding the wave of people. We find our car buried inside the parking lot, completely boxed in. I unlock it and we climb inside, but we're not going anywhere anytime soon.

"I think we freaked out that guy who was sitting next to me," I say. "He kept glancing over at us like he was afraid we might start ripping each other's clothes off or something."

"I bet he was hoping we would," Ben says.

"I think he was more anxious than interested," I say.

"We probably should have waited until we were alone before we made out like that," Ben says.

"That wasn't making out. We were just kissing."

Ben looks into my eyes. "That wasn't 'just kissing.'"

While it's true that all we did was kiss, Ben is right. Those kisses were infused with so much passion, that they really weren't just ordinary kisses.

I have the sudden urge to be close to Ben. I climb over the console and squeeze into his seat with him.

"Who said you could come over here?" Ben asks, in a mock-stern tone.

"I'll go back to my seat if you want me to," I say, pushing myself up.

Ben pulls me to him. "No, I want you to stay right here."

I snuggle against his chest, breathing in his clean, sweet scent. "I want to make love with you," I whisper into his t-shirt. The instant the words leave my mouth, I can't believe I said them. But then again, I can. I feel like I can say anything to Ben. And do anything with him. Even make love. And I feel like I *need* to make love with Ben. Like my life won't be complete without it.

Ben pulls away. "We can't do that."

"You don't want to?" I ask, surprised by his reaction.

He looks into my eyes. "Of course I do, but …"

"But what?"

Ben rubs his forehead and turns away without answering.

"What, Ben?" I ask.

After a moment, he turns back to me. His eyes brim with tears. "From the moment we met, you've been worried about me hurting you. Have you ever stopped to think that *you* might hurt *me*?"

No, I haven't. In the past few weeks, I haven't thought much about other people's needs. It's not that I don't want to; it's just that I've needed every ounce of my energy just to survive.

It kills me to think of causing Ben any pain. But I wonder if it's too late now to prevent that. Our connection has become so deep that, when we are forced to separate, I think the hurt will be inevitable.

"Why in the world would you want us to make love?" Ben asks, shaking his head.

"Because … I want to make a lifetime of memories with you, even if that means the pain will be worse in the end." I take a deep breath, willing my tears to stay in my eyes, where they are. But I lose the battle and they fall down my cheeks.

A hand raps on the driver's side window.

"Do you mind moving your car?" the man says through the glass.

I jump back into the driver's seat and slide the key into the ignition.

Ben fastens his seatbelt and closes his eyes. "Just tell the GPS to take us home."

I turn on the GPS and tell it, "Go home."

We drive all the way back to Ben's house in complete silence.

Except for the calm, menacing voice of Darth Vader.

Chapter Eleven

I awaken to a scratching sound coming from outside the guest room. In a sleepy haze, I check the bottom of the door for the cat toy/intruder detector. But then I realize I didn't put it there last night. My heart sinks when I remember the reason: I figure Ben has absolutely no interest in entering my room now. I think about our last conversation, and a knot of regret forms in my gut. I don't regret what I wanted; I still want to make love with Ben—even now. But I regret that telling him made him so upset.

Outside the door, I find Bolt. I sit on the floor, scoop him into my lap, and kiss the soft fur behind his ears, listening to his purr, along with the soft clicking of the keys of Ben's laptop. When Bolt hops off my lap, I drag myself to my feet and down the hallway. I pause at Ben's open doorway and watch him type just as fast as he did in the coffee shop. Based on the passionate concentration on his face, I feel certain that, unlike then, now he is actually writing a story. After a few minutes of him not noticing me—or ignoring me—I go to the kitchen.

The TV is on, but I barely pay attention to it as I eat my almond butter and granola. After a few minutes, Ben joins me in the kitchen. He grabs a glass and fills it with water.

"How's the writing going?" I ask.

"Good."

"I'm sorry about what I said in the car last night." I never thought I'd apologize to a man for wanting to have sex with him.

"It's okay."

"You probably wish I never sat down at your table in the coffee shop."

Ben sets his glass on the counter. Without speaking, he walks over to me and takes me into his arms. He holds me close for a long time before he whispers, "I would have been devastated if you didn't."

Ben strokes my hair, sending shivers through me that I can't suppress. I lift my head to look at him and our lips meet, at first lightly and tentatively, but together they grow strong and certain. Ben's body presses against mine. I feel his heart beat against my chest. His strong hands hold me tight.

The longer we kiss, the more I feel like he might be changing his mind about something.

And the more I want him to.

Suddenly, Ben pulls back. "We've got a lot to do today. We should probably get going."

I inhale, trying to regain control of my brain. "Okay."

* * *

Our hike in Malibu Creek State Park begins in golden, rolling meadows. We follow a duck-inhabited creek to a path lined by thick trees that meet above our heads, creating a ceiling of tangled branches. The trail rises and then descends into a pine forest, where we see two young deer grazing among the tall trees. The animals stay just long enough for me to snap a picture.

After we cross a swampy stream, we amble along a boulder-strewn trail that opens into a shrubby area surrounded by tree-covered hills and rocky mountains.

"We're here!" Ben points to an old-fashioned army ambulance parked in the dry grass alongside the dirt trail. Other than the fact that its rusted wheels have lost their tires, the ambulance appears ready for its next patient. Ben grabs my hand. "Come on. There's more!"

We continue along the trail until we arrive at a large clearing. There are two more vehicles here, but unlike the ambulance, they are thoroughly rusted and sagging. In a former life, one might have been an ambulance. The other, a jeep.

"We are now standing in the exact spot where they filmed *M*A*S*H*," Ben announces.

Wooden plaques that display photos from the TV show are scattered throughout the clearing. Looking up from the photos, I recognize the rutted mountains. The elaborate *M*A*S*H* sets are long gone, but the mountains have changed only a little over the years.

"And check this out!" Ben says, racing up a steep trail.

I follow him to where the trail ends, in an unremarkable flat area covered in twisted shrubs.

"On the TV show, this was the helicopter landing area," Ben says, then his gaze rises to take in our surroundings, and he adds, "It's one of my favorite spots in the world."

I see what he means: the brown-green mountains, the clear blue sky, the abandoned cars below. It's beautiful, in a way. Unique. Different from anyplace else I've seen in Los Angeles. Different from any place I've ever been.

Ben holds out his hand. "Would you like to dance?"

I stare at his hand for a moment, remembering the first time he offered it to me. I'd been too afraid to touch him then, too afraid to trust him. But now, without any apprehension, I accept his hand. Ben places his other one on my hip and begins to hum a slow, melancholy tune.

"That's a pretty song," I say after a minute.

"It's the *M*A*S*H* theme song," Ben says. "It's called 'Suicide is Painless.'" And then he starts humming it again.

And so we dance our first—and probably our last—slow-dance.

To "Suicide is Painless."

* * *

In a valley of towering, craggy, black boulders, Ben and I sit on a large rock at the edge of the mirrored pond that Ben calls "*Planet of the Apes* Lake," because it's where they filmed some scenes for the original movie.

All of a sudden, on a flat rock across the pond, I see Star. She stands there with her piercing blue eyes staring at me and her forehead deeply furrowed. I don't recall her looking at me this way in life, but in death it is the only expression I ever see from her.

"Is something wrong?" Ben asks me.

"I was thinking about Star," I say. And then I admit, "Sometimes, I imagine that I see her."

"You see her now?" he asks.

"Over there." I raise my finger and point, even though it makes no sense to do so.

Ben glances at where I point. His eyes narrow as he turns back to me. I feel like he's trying hard to fight the conclusion that I'm insane.

"Do you think I'm crazy?" I ask.

"I think you're dealing with a lot of difficult stuff."

I exhale, feeling slightly more normal. "Whenever I see her, she always looks so angry."

"What do you think she's angry about?" Ben asks.

I take a deep breath, trying to convince myself that I

can tell Ben this, trying to convince myself that he'll understand. Finally, I say, "It's my fault she's dead."

"How is it your fault?" Ben asks.

I focus on the algae-covered rocks beneath the surface of the water. "Star's parents went away one weekend. She told me she wouldn't be able to hang out with me because she was going to spend all day Saturday and Sunday studying—she tended to do that before big tests. On Saturday morning, I baked some peanut butter cookies. Star loved peanut butter cookies, so I went to her house to drop some off. She always did that kind of thing for me.

"When I got there, I heard a car running in the garage, but the door was closed. I used the security code to open the garage door. And I found Star sitting in the driver's seat of her dad's car. Her eyes were open, but there wasn't any life left in them. I dragged her out of the car and did CPR on her, but it was already too late.

"The police found a suicide note in Star's room, but her parents wouldn't let me read it. I think they blamed me for Star's death." Tears slip down my cheeks. "I was her best friend. How could I not have known she was hurting? How could I not have stopped her from killing herself?"

I look up at Star, but her gaze falls away from mine.

"If someone wants you to stop them, they give you a chance," Ben says very softly.

I look at him. "Did *you* give someone a chance to stop you?"

"No," he says simply.

"So you really wanted to die?" I ask.

"That day when I went to my father's office … It was a Sunday morning. I planned it so my father would find me on Monday, when he came in to work. By then I would be long dead. I didn't know there was a weekend janitor. That's who found me. The janitor." He swallows and looks into my eyes. "Star didn't want anyone to stop her."

"And neither did you," I say, sadness rising within me.

"I thought there was nothing good left for me in life. I was *certain* of that," Ben says. "But I was wrong."

I look to see if Star has a response to Ben's words, but she is gone.

Chapter Twelve

I drive along a narrow road flanked by a rocky hillside and a deserted white-sand beach. Darth Vader informed us that we arrived at our destination a few minutes ago. Now he is vehemently insisting that we turn back. Ben tells me to keep driving, so I silence Darth and drive until we run out of pavement. I park inches from the beach.

Ben pops out of the car. "Race ya," he says.

He takes off, sprinting toward the ominous, churning ocean. I run after him through the hot sand.

Ben stops below a sheer cliff that rock climbers have strung with ropes—turning it into a playground for the fearless. He waits for me to catch up. When I do, I look for the tide pools that Ben promised we would see here, but I only see furious waves pounding at the sand.

"Where are the tide pools?" I ask.

"They're on the other side of the bluff, but there's something I want to show you first."

Ben leads me to where the cliff plunges into the ocean. He scrambles onto the tall mound of boulders there and I cautiously follow. My focus alternates between watching my footing on the treacherous path and glancing at the too-close, menacing water.

When I can finally peer over the boulders ahead of us, I see what looks like the shore of a deserted island. The small half-moon-shaped beach, tucked into the bottom of the cliff, shows no evidence that humans have ever explored it. There's not one footprint on the pristine sand. Ben takes my hand to help me with my final steps down from the boulders and doesn't let go as we make our way toward the water.

Anxiety chills my skin. My pulse rises. I pull away. "Ben, I ... I'm scared."

"Of what?" he asks.

"The ocean."

Ben stands between me and the ocean, as if he's protecting me from it. "Because of Alexis?"

I nod. "I used to love swimming in the ocean. It made me feel so calm. Now, even if I just look at it, all I feel is terror."

"You don't have to do anything you don't want to do," Ben says. "But if you *want* to swim in the ocean again, you *can*. I promise you that."

I'm not sure if I want to feel the power of the ocean again, but I slip off my shoes and socks. Ben slips off his, and then, tightly gripping Ben's hand, I lead him to where the water touches the shore. A wave licks my toes. Its icy coolness burns like flames from a fire. I plant my feet and let another wave scald me. And then another, and another.

When the next one comes, I hardly feel it. I'm not sure whether the pain has dissipated or my body has grown numb. I take one step into the water. A wave washes over my calves. I feel its chill.

I'm not numb.

I look into Ben's dark eyes. "I want to go in all the way." I feel like if I don't do this right here, right now, I will never get a chance again. I feel like might be able to do this, but only with Ben.

"Are you sure?" he asks.

"Yes."

I go back to the beach, lift my shirt up over my head and lay it on the sand, shivering as the ocean air tickles my skin. Ben pulls off his own shirt and drops it next to mine. I slide off my shorts and he slides off his too. And then, in our underwear, we walk back to the water.

Ben and I go deeper and deeper into the deadly ocean, so deep that our feet can't touch the sand. I close my eyes and let myself sink down into the water. When I come up for air, I open my eyes and find Ben watching over me. Making sure I stay safe. I feel like nothing bad can happen to me with Ben by my side. I close my eyes again and force myself to surrender to the water. I let it take me. But only for a while.

When Ben and I finally climb back onto the warm sand, we sit and stare at the ocean.

It doesn't look so deadly anymore.

* * *

According to Ben, the cliffside trail that we follow leads to the tide pools. The path becomes more and more rugged as we descend. By the time we arrive at the metal staircase that leads down to the beach, I'm not surprised to find it rusted all the way through in places. I grip the railing tightly, taking each step one at a time, until we land safely in the sand.

Ben dashes ahead of me toward the rocky shore. He stops and crouches down to peer into the water that has pooled between some lumpy black rocks. I squat down by his side and gaze into the water, but I see only sand, nothing of any interest. We move to another pool and find sand, rocks, and a bit of seaweed.

"This isn't how I remember them." Ben shakes his head and moves on to another pool.

Just before I stand, something in the pool of water at my feet comes out from under the seaweed: a little shell. Tiny crab claws along the bottom of the shell and carry it across the floor of the pool. I reach down and take the shell into my hand. It sits there for a minute, lifeless, and then the crab emerges again.

"Don't drop him," a woman says from behind me. She sounds as if she's talking to a young child.

I squint my eyes against the sunlight and see a woman standing over me. Her long brown hair falls to either side of her face. I recognize her from photos of my past, photos of me as a baby, photos of moments I don't remember experiencing.

"I won't, Mommy," I hear myself say, but my voice is that of a little girl.

I look back at my hands. They are no longer the hands I know; they are those of a very small child. I cup them together to give the crab more room to crawl around.

"Good girl, Erin," the woman says. "You're such a good girl."

I look up at her again, but see only sunlight. I look down and see the crab scurry across my fully-grown adult hands. Someone kneels next to me. Ben.

"What'd you find?" he asks.

"A hermit crab," I say, tears blurring my vision. "And a memory."

Until just a moment ago, I didn't have any memories of my mother. I had stories that I forcefully extracted from my father, a few photos, and one video clip of my mother and me riding a merry-go-round, but I had no actual recollections of having known her. I often wondered what she sounded like, and whether her personality was anything like mine—because my personality isn't much like my father's.

"What'd you remember?" Ben asks.

"Being a little girl. I was with my mother. I was holding a hermit crab, and she told me not to drop him." I sigh. "I wish I could remember more."

I slip the hermit crab back into the tide pool where I found him, wipe my eyes on the back of my hand, and Ben and I continue along the beach until we spot another collection of tide pools. We bend down next to the first pool.

Ben brightens and points to something purple below a shelf of rock. "There's a starfish!" Then he gestures to clusters of little green tentacles extending from one wall of the pool. "And tons of anemones!" He exhales, appearing relieved. "*This* is the kind of tide pool I remember."

For the next hour, we go from tide pool to tide pool, admiring anemones, large and small. And starfish as big as Ben's hands, yellow ones, pink ones, and purple ones. And many, many hermit crabs. The pools are truly mesmerizing. Like an underwater world.

But none of these other tide pools offer anything as wonderful as what I found in that second tide pool. The one with the lone hermit crab ... and a memory from my childhood.

* * *

From the top of the cliff overlooking the nearly-submerged

half-moon beach, Ben and I watch the sun set on our final day together. We sit close to each other, our bodies almost touching.

"Do you still want to make love?" Ben asks, his tone more curious than seductive.

I swallow. "Here?"

"Someplace where we wouldn't get arrested," Ben says. "I mean, have you changed your mind?"

"No." Ben is the first guy I've ever actually loved. My "first time" was taken from me. I want my second time to be with Ben.

"What if it hurts you?" he asks.

I don't know if he means physically or emotionally, but either way ... "It probably will."

He shakes his head. "Then *why* do you want to do it?"

I inhale, and then I speak with my heart rather than my head. "I've exposed my soul to you in a way that I've never allowed it to be exposed to anyone else in my entire life. I feel like making love to you would let our souls touch. I want that to happen. I *need* that to happen."

Ben doesn't respond.

We sit in silence as the fiery sliver of sun grows smaller and smaller as it falls into the ocean.

When it is gone, Ben finally turns toward me.

His face is streaked with tears.

Chapter Thirteen

Because of the traffic, it takes about two hours to drive from Malibu to Hollywood. Ben and I fill the time with small talk, occasionally interrupted by Darth Vader's breathy directions. Whenever there's a lull in the conversation, I think about what will happen once we're back at Ben's house. My body tingles when I imagine us alone, free to do whatever we want with each other, whatever feels right.

When we turn onto the street with the coffee shop where Ben and I met, a bubble of sadness rises in my chest. *Maybe we should have a final cup of coffee there tomorrow morning, before I go.*

Or maybe that would be too heartbreaking.

We are almost at Ben's street when he asks, "Still up for the observatory?"

The observatory was on our itinerary for tonight, but I

thought, after our conversation on the cliff as we watched the sun set, that our plans had changed. I guess they haven't.

"Um. Okay," I say.

I silence Darth. I know the way from here.

* * *

The observatory doesn't feel nearly as claustrophobic as it did the last time I visited, even though there are easily twice as many people here tonight. It helps that I have Ben's hand to hold.

A woman announces over the PA system that the final planetarium show of the evening is about to begin. Ben and I rush to buy our tickets and then head into the theater to find some seats. As we settle into the semi-reclined, cushioned chairs, I realize how utterly exhausted I am. I'm ready to drift off into a contented nap, when the theater disappears, replaced by the night sky. My eyes widen and I stare up at the stars, suddenly feeling very small.

I think about Ben and me. How we are two tiny sentient specks of dust in the universe. Two tiny specks who love each other. Yes, I'm certain that Ben loves me the way I love him. It is the kind of love that I thought I'd never get the chance to experience in my life, not even for a moment. It hurts my heart to know that, less than twenty-four hours from now, Ben and I will be over two thousand miles apart.

My only comfort is that, when you consider the entire universe, that isn't very far at all.

* * *

After the planetarium show is over, Ben and I head outside and climb a twisting, narrow staircase to go for a look through the massive Zeiss telescope on the roof of the observatory. When I gaze through the eyepiece, I feel incredibly close to the moon, much closer than I did when I looked through the smaller telescope on the observatory lawn. This telescope is so powerful that I can see little details in the moon's craters. Seeing their sharp rims, steep walls, and shadowed, bumpy floors makes the moon feel more like a real place, like someplace I could actually hike around and touch. Of course, for an ordinary person, hiking on the moon is impossible, but as I gaze through that telescope, it feels possible.

When I finally exit the telescope room, I walk to the edge of the observatory roof, toward the tiny glittering lights of nighttime Los Angeles. Like the planetarium show, the far-away city lights make me feel small. I am lost in my thoughts when Ben comes up behind me and wraps his arms around me. Instantly, I feel big again. It's as if the tiny bit of universe that holds Ben and me has suddenly expanded.

And in that moment, I make a decision.

* * *

I wait until Ben and I are resting side-by-side on one of the lounge chairs by his pool, staring up at the stars, before I say, "I realized something tonight."

He smiles. "What?"

I look into his eyes. I trust them completely. "I need to stay here."

"What do you mean?" he asks, looking confused.

"I've decided to stay in Los Angeles," I say.

Pain crosses Ben's face. He stiffens. "No."

For a while, I don't breathe. What could he possibly mean by that? I wait for an explanation, but he doesn't offer one. Finally, I ask, "No, *what*?"

"You need to go back to New York," he says. "Your whole life is there."

I can't believe what he's saying. "I thought you wanted us to be together."

"We both knew this was only temporary."

'Temporary'? I never thought a single word could break my heart. "Is that what this was to you? I was some girl you could have a little fun with and then never see again?" Suddenly, I hate Ben. *I hate him.*

He runs his fingers through his hair. "I didn't want it to end like this."

"Like what? With you telling me this was 'only temporary'? Yeah, Ben, that *is* a rotten way to end things."

"No. I didn't want this to end with us in love with each

other."

I hate him. "You don't love me."

Tears form in his eyes. "Yes, I do," he whispers.

"If you love me, why don't you want me to stay with you?"

He looks deep into my eyes. "Someday you'll understand."

"What?" I demand. "What will I understand? Tell me, Ben."

He just shakes his head.

I close my eyes, forcing back the tears that are begging to come. My heart hurts so badly that I feel as if it is about to burst open. I hate Ben. I hate him for not telling me why he doesn't want to be with me. And I hate him for not wanting to be with me. *Whatever* the reason is. But at the same time I love him. I love him in a way that I've never loved anyone before. I can't figure out how to hold both of those feelings inside me. I have to let one go. The love or the hate. It is the only way for me to survive this.

I decide to make the terrifying choice, the dangerous choice, the choice that could destroy me if my decision is the wrong one. But it is the only choice I can live with.

I decide to let go of the hate.

"I'm going to tell you a secret," I say. "Something I haven't told anyone. Something I wasn't sure I was ever going to tell you. I was just going to show you. But I might not get the chance to show you now. And I can't leave without telling you this."

Ben doesn't look at me. He stares at the stars. "Okay."

"When I got back to New York, I was planning to climb over the railing of the Brooklyn Bridge, and dive into the East River. And die."

He still doesn't look at me. His expression is stoic. Unreadable.

"Why didn't you tell me that before?" he asks.

"I guess … Initially, because I didn't want you to try to stop me. And then later, because I didn't want to hurt you."

"So you're ready to hurt me now."

"No. I'm telling you now because I don't want to die anymore. Because of you, Ben. Because of how I love you. With my entire heart. With my soul. I never thought it would be possible for me to love someone that way again. That completely. But I still can. Despite everything painful that's happened in my past, despite everything painful that will happen in my future, I'll never stop being able to love. Because you showed me how."

Ben takes me into his arms and holds me tightly for a long time.

We're both trembling when he finally pulls away. "Let's go for a swim," he whispers.

He pulls his t-shirt over his head. I unbutton my shirt and slip it off. Ben unzips his shorts. I open my bra and let it fall onto the chair. I slide my shorts off, followed by my panties. Ben must be fully undressed now, but I don't look at him. Instead, I turn and dive into the pool. The cold water courses over every inch of my skin. It feels freeing. I take a breath at the surface and then let myself sink all the way down to the bottom.

Ben plunges into the water next to me. I watch his naked body fall in a net of bubbles and then rise slightly. His hair dances, weightless, above his head. We stare at each other through the water for a moment, then I grab a breath and take off toward the opposite end of the pool. I swim hard and fast to the wall, then stop and twirl around. Ben is right behind me. I race past him, back to the other end of the pool, stopping only for a quick gasp of air. Ben pursues me. He grabs my foot. I yank it from his grasp, push off the bottom of the pool, and splash to the surface, breathing hard. Ben surfaces next to me. His breaths are heavy. He eases me against the edge of the pool, his body pressed to mine. Our lips meet without hesitation. Full of desire and desperation. As Ben draws me closer, I feel something slip between my legs. And then I realize: *It's going to happen.*

"We need protection," I breathe.

"I'll be right back." Ben's muscles tense as he climbs out of the pool. He runs to the house.

I climb out of the water and sit on a lounge chair, my pulse pounding. A breeze hits my wet skin. I shiver from its chill.

"Here," Ben says, reappearing by my side. He holds out a small box that is shrink-wrapped in cellophane.

"Did you buy that for us?" I ask.

He sits on another lounge chair, facing me. "No. It was a gift."

"A gift?"

"From a girl in my cancer support group," Ben explains. "She said that when a guy gets cancer he can expect certain 'pity-perks.' I think she was making an offer. I didn't take her up on it."

"Why not?"

"I was waiting for the right girl."

I never considered the possibility that Ben hadn't done this before. "Are you a—?"

His cheeks redden. "Yeah, so don't expect much."

"I don't want you to regret your first time," I say, inching away from him. "You should wait until you find the right girl."

"I found her. I just can't keep her." Ben looks deep into my eyes, leaving me confident that his words are the truth. "I want to make love with you, Erin," he continues. "More than anything in the universe."

No matter where my life goes from here, I am certain that I will never regret what I am about to do. I guide Ben back onto the lounge chair, and he takes me with him. Gravity holds us together. Our lips meet once again, and his breaths become mine. His hands run over my back, pressing deeply, pushing our hungry bodies together. We kiss, our bodies sliding against one another until I neither of us can wait any longer.

Ben unwraps the little box. I lie back and close my eyes. My heart pounds as I brace for the pain.

Suddenly, the air is heavy. *I can't breathe.* My eyes spring open.

"Are you sure you're ready for this?" Ben asks.

"Yes." I take a deep breath. *I have to be ready. This is my only chance.*

I guide Ben into me. It hurts, but not nearly as much as I expected it would. He closes his eyes, but I keep my eyes open. I need to look at Ben to stay calm.

As he enters me deeper and deeper, my body relaxes. Pleasure rises inside me. And an aching to have him inside me deeper still. I feel as if any distance between us is too great. As I let him enter me completely, Ben's face grows intense, as if he's studying for a test. And then, he winces.

"Don't move," he whispers.

"Are you okay?"

"I'm ... really, really good!" Ben says. And then he asks, "Are you okay?"

"Yes, I'm okay."

I lace my fingers with his and finally let my eyes close. Every cell in my body focuses on the joy of being with Ben. Our bodies moving together. It is our second slow-dance—and now, almost certainly, our last. But this dance lasts only seconds before he releases into me, and waves of warm energy surge through me. For those moments, I can't think; I can only feel.

And then it's over.

Our bodies go limp, except for our hearts, which pound within our chests.

Ben kisses me gently. "I told you not to expect much."

I try to respond, but it's hard to talk.

I can't imagine anything ever being better than that.

Chapter Fourteen

I wake up where I remember falling asleep: in Ben's bed. I remember lying wrapped in his arms, trying desperately to stay awake so I could experience every remaining moment we had together. But my eyelids became heavier and heavier. I finally had to shut them, just to rest for a few minutes. That's the last thing I remember until now.

Ben's laptop sits, closed, on his desk. I hug his pillow and breath in deeply, inhaling the clean, sweet scent that is only his. Even though I've had just a few hours of sleep, I hop out of bed. Bolt comes running to greet me and purrs enthusiastically as I pet him.

"Where's Ben?" I ask Bolt.

The TV chatters away in the kitchen. I go to there, expecting to find Ben at the kitchen table having some tea. But he isn't there. I look through the sliding-glass windows, into the backyard, and find the yard deserted. I walk back down the hallway, listening for signs of life upstairs. "Ben?" I call up the stairway. There's no answer.

He must have run out to get something. I hope he isn't gone long. I only have a few hours left until my airport shuttle will be here. But he knows that.

I decide to have some breakfast—my usual almond butter and granola concoction—and watch the news. As the meteorologist talks about the sunny forecast for the next seven days, all I can think is that I won't be in Los Angeles tomorrow. I don't know when I will return. Or even if I'll ever come back here. I lump of sadness forms in my throat, but I swallow it away. The meteorologist finishes with his forecast and hands the program back to one of the anchors. Two photos appear over her left shoulder: a photo of a middle-aged woman and a photo of a little girl with golden curls.

I stop eating so that I don't choke.

I know those people. I met them a few days ago, during my solo visit to Griffith Observatory.

The anchor tells the story, "The Los Angeles County Coroner's office has confirmed that the bodies of a woman and a child found inside a burned-out car in Griffith Park are that of four-year-old Eliza Frend and her non-custodial parent, Rebecca Long …"

My brain fills with horror. I can't believe that what she says is true. *How can Eliza be dead?* I just saw her, vibrant and alive, four days ago. *How can she be gone?*

The anchor continues, "The car was discovered by park rangers fourteen days ago, just hours after the child was reported missing from her father's home."

Fourteen days ago? That must be wrong. I saw them *four* days ago. They stood right next to me.

My vision blurs. My skin grows cold.

Where is Ben? I need Ben.

My entire body shakes, as I make my way down the hallway and check Ben's room again.

He's still not there.

I run upstairs and poke my head into each doorway. "BEN! BEN! BEN!"

I race back downstairs and into the backyard. "BEN!"

Anxiety builds in my gut. I check the hot tub and the pool. "BEN!"

Ben, where are you? I need you.

My head feels light and dizzy. I go back into Ben's room and lie down on his bed, staring at model of the solar system on the ceiling. *He'll be back soon*, I tell myself. *He'll be back soon.* I lie there, repeating that over and over until I calm down.

I need to keep busy until he comes back. I decide to upload the photos on my camera to Ben's computer, to surprise him. I turn on Ben's laptop and a password screen comes up.

I try the only possible password I can think of: bolt.

That is incorrect.

I highlight the "b" and change it to "B."

I'm in!

I connect my camera to the laptop, and my photos appear on the screen as tiny thumbnails. I select them all and drop them into a folder that I name "Ben and Erin." Then I click "Slide show."

The first photo fills the entire screen: celebrity hand and footprints. It's blurry. *I don't remember taking that one.* The next one is me with the footprints. It must be the one taken by the Japanese tourist. But Ben is missing from the photo. *He must have stepped away at the last moment. But why would he do that?* The next photo is me with the Hollywood Sign in the distance, just me, no Ben, even though I'd thought Ben was right next to me when the photo was taken.

I click through photo after photo. Not one of them includes Ben.

How did he avoid being in every single picture?

I go to the living room. To the photos on the mantle. I never bothered looking at them before. Now, I study them. Ben is in every one: Ben graduating from preschool, Ben at a park, Ben riding a horse. There's a photo of young Ben with a smiling man and woman. I assume they're his parents. I stare at the eyes of the man. *He doesn't look like a monster.* But monsters don't always look like monsters.

I find a photo that looks recent. Of Ben standing in

front of Griffith Observatory. I stuff it into my backpack and sprint out the door. I run down the street, then I race the few blocks to the coffee shop. I compose myself as best I can and go inside.

I scan the tables. Ben isn't here.

I go to the counter, and the same girl who was working here on my other visits greets me.

"Erin, right?" she asks.

I nod.

"The usual?" she asks.

"Just the coffee. No muffin."

A moment later she places a coffee on the counter.

I hand her two dollars, but instead of taking the coffee, I reach into my backpack and pull out Ben's picture. "Do you know him?" I ask her.

She smiles as if she is looking at a sad puppy. "Ben. Yeah."

"Has he been in here today?" I ask.

"How did you know him?" she asks without answering.

'Did'? I freeze. "Why did you say 'did'?"

"Ben died a few months ago," she says softly.

My heart nearly stops. Because I know deep inside that what she says is true. *Ben is dead.*

My voice barely comes. "What did he die of?"

"Leukemia."

I walk away from the counter and sit at the table where

Ben and I once sat. The girl brings my coffee and sets it in front of me, but I don't touch it. Instead, I focus on my breathing. In and out. I feel like, if I don't consciously breathe, I won't breathe at all. I am numb and empty. Lost and confused. And yet now everything makes sense.

These past few days, I was the only one who felt Ben's presence. Ben impacted only me, nothing and no one else. But I hadn't questioned it. I had suspended all disbelief. I had accepted with my entire soul that Ben was here with me. Because I needed an angel.

* * *

Nothing has changed in the universe. Ben was dead when I "met" him. Still, I mourn my loss. The only way to close the distance between us is for me to die. And I no longer want to die.

Bolt follows me through Ben's house, as I return Ben's photo to the mantle, delete the "Ben and Erin" folder from Ben's laptop, pack my belongings, and straighten up, trying to leave no trace of my visit.

I go to turn off the still-chattering TV in the kitchen and notice something by the plug: a timer. *The TV will turn itself off, and it will turn itself on again tomorrow.* I don't disturb it.

I stop by the mantle one last time. For a moment, I consider whether Ben's mom would miss that one photo of Ben at the observatory. But I don't take it; it isn't mine to take. Instead, I pull out my camera and take a photo of the photo. It's the closest thing to a picture of Ben that I will ever have.

As I slip my camera back into its case, another photo on the mantle catches my attention. I pick it up, and I'm forced to sit on the floor because my legs have gone limp. The photo is of two women and two children on a beach. The first woman has long brown hair. She is wearing the same yellow blouse that she wore in my only memory of her. *My mother.* Nestled in her lap is a tiny version of me—about three years old. Next to us is Ben's mom. On her lap is an adorable little Ben. Ben and I are holding hands and smiling broad smiles. I stare at our small hands. Touching.

I'm not sure whether the Ben I knew over the past few days was an angel, or a ghost, or a hallucination. But this photo is real. It is proof that, long before he died, Ben and I knew each other. We once held hands.

I carefully aim my camera—wishing that I could stop my hands from shaking—and take a photo of the photo. Then I kiss Bolt goodbye, hide the spare house key in the squirrel statue, and go sit on the curb with my suitcase to wait for the airport shuttle. The shuttle isn't supposed to come for another hour, but I can't bear to stay in Ben's home any longer without him.

* * *

About thirty minutes after I sit down on the curb, a town car pulls up. I wonder if the shuttle company made a mistake and sent a town car for me instead of a van, until the driver opens the back door and Ben's mom climbs out. The driver sets her large suitcase on the sidewalk. She tips him and heads toward the house, wheeling the suitcase behind her.

I stand and hear myself say, "Excuse me, ma'am. I'm Erin Winters." I'm not sure if she will recognize my name, but it is the only thing I can think of to say.

She turns and looks at me for what feels like ages. Then she abandons her bag on the walkway, rushes over, and throws her arms around me. She hugs me for an eternity, and then she stares at me in disbelief. "Would you like to come in?" she finally asks.

I've never gone through the front door of Ben's house before. At least not that I remember. Bolt greets us there. I stroke him on the head and he purrs.

Ben's mom invites me to sit on the couch. "How did you find me?" she asks.

"It's a long story" *that I can't really explain and still sound sane* "and I only have a few minutes before my airport shuttle gets here." I take a breath. "I know you knew my mother and me. Did you know us well?"

Ben's mom appears puzzled. "Your mom and I were best friends since high school."

Ben's mother was my mother's best friend. I think of the questions that have been haunting me practically my whole life. I don't know if this woman has any answers, but there's a chance she might, and so I start, "My mother left me and my father fourteen years ago—"

"I know," she says.

She knows. "Do you know *why* she left us?"

"I'm not sure."

"But you have some idea." I sense from her answer.

"Your mother loved you very much, but she wasn't ready to settle down and be a mommy. She had a restless soul. She dreamed of traveling the world."

Hope floods into me. "Do you know where she is now?"

"For years, I tried to find her, but my searches always turned up empty."

I exhale every shred of hope I was holding onto. For a moment, I had allowed myself to think that maybe this woman held the answer I've been looking for all these years. But she doesn't. I blink away the tears forming in my eyes. The clock is ticking away on my time here. "Could you tell me about my mother?"

"I can do better than that." Ben's mom leaps up from the couch with renewed energy. A minute later, she returns with a thick photo album that has a map of the world on the cover. She places it on my lap and opens it. On the first page are more photos of my mother than I've ever seen in one place. Photos of Ben's mother and my mother as young teenagers, at the beach. These photos are so much better than the few I have. My mother looks happier than I've ever seen her, and I can see the details of her face. Her long eyelashes. Her light freckles. I recognize myself in her.

I page through the album, looking at the photos: holidays, birthdays, hanging out, clowning around. Then there's a photo of my mother and Ben's mother lounging on the lawn in front of Griffith Observatory, and another one of them posing with the Hollywood Sign, and one of them standing on a footbridge that arches over a canal. There is a gray-haired woman in the background of the canal photo; she's painting a mural on the fence of a fairytale cottage.

Ben's mom explains, "Your mom and I took a trip to L.A. when we were teenagers." She points to the painter in the canal photo. "That woman painted us into her mural." She turns the page and I see them posing with the same mural I stumbled on in Venice a few days ago, the mural that I'd thought at first glance featured Star and me. *The brown-haired girl in the mural was my mom.*

A few pages later, Ben's mom and my mom each have a tiny baby in their arms. "That's you," Ben's mom says pointing to the infant in my mom's arms. Then she points to the other infant. "And that's my son, Ben. You two were inseparable from the moment you met."

The photos before me document the life Ben and I once shared. Infant Ben and me, his baby fist clutching my tiny finger. Ben and me fast asleep, side-by-side in a blue playpen. Hugging an enormous pumpkin. Riding on a sled in the snow. Page after page, as I watch us grow into best friends, I see the light fade from my mom's eyes, and her smile becomes weary. After a while, my mom disappears from the photos. She must have been too tired to force a smile.

The final photo in the book shows toddler Ben giving me a kiss on the cheek as I grin delightedly. I can't stop looking at the photo.

"He loved you," Ben's mom says. "I wish you and Ben could get to know each other again. But he passed away two months ago."

Even though I already knew this, her words hit me like a blow to the chest. It's as if looking at these photos brought Ben back to life; now her words plummet me back into reality.

"Do you remember him?" Ben's mom asks.

"I will never, ever forget him."

I didn't cry when I found out Ben was dead. Now I cry so hard that my whole body shakes. Ben's mom takes me in her arms protectively. She's crying too.

A minute later, my phone rings. The airport shuttle driver is here.

"Hold on," Ben's mom says as she dashes off again. An instant later, she returns with a small book titled "Ben and Erin." On the cover is the photo of Ben, me, and our moms that I saw on the mantle. "I made this for Ben when he was a little boy," Ben's mom says. "I think he'd want you to have it."

"Thank you," I say, my eyes filling with tears again.

She scribbles something on a notepad and then hands me the paper. "Here's my phone number and email address. Please keep in touch, Erin."

"I will," I say.

And then I realize why Ben brought me here.

* * *

I wait until I'm safely ensconced in my cramped airline seat and my seatmate has drifted off to sleep before I remove Ben's book from my backpack and open it. Inside the front cover is a sticker that says "This book belongs to" with a line under it. On the line, in big blue crayon letters, is scrawled "Ben," with a backward "B." I smile, imagining little Ben carefully printing his name in the book.

I turn to the first photo-filled page and read:

Ben and Erin:
The Tale of Two Forever Friends

By Mommy

Ben and Erin were born on the very same day,
in the very same hospital,
in the very same room.

Their mommies were best friends.

Ben and Erin were best friends too.

Ben and Erin visited each other almost every day.

They went for walks in Central Park,

and to see the stars at Hayden Planetarium,

and to play in the waves at Jones Beach.

They had many, many, many adventures together.

One day, Ben's family had to move to California.

Ben was sad that Erin couldn't come with him ...

But then Erin came for a visit!

They went for walks in Malibu Creek State Park,

and to explore the tide pools at Point Dume Beach,

and to look through the big telescope at Griffith Observatory.

They made many, many, many memories.

When it was time for Erin to go home,

Ben and Erin put all of those memories in their hearts,

for safe keeping.

They knew they would see each other again someday.

Because Ben and Erin were forever friends.

The final two words have been scribbled out by firm strokes of blue crayon. They are barely legible:

The End

About the author

J.W. Lynne has been an avid reader practically since birth and now writes inventive novels with twists, turns, and surprises. In addition to LOST IN LOS ANGELES, Lynne is the author of LOST IN TOKYO, which picks up Erin's journey one year later. In Lynne's science fiction trilogy (ABOVE THE SKY, RETURN TO THE SKY, and PART OF THE SKY), an eighteen-year-old fights to survive in a dystopian future society founded on lies. KID DOCS dives into the behind-the-scenes action at a hospital where gifted young children are trained to become pint-sized doctors. In WILD ANIMAL SCHOOL, a teen spends an unforgettable summer working with elephants, tigers, bears, leopards, and lions at an exotic animal ranch.

Printed in Great Britain
by Amazon